Ten

Juan Emar

TEN

*translated from the Spanish
by Megan McDowell*

with an introduction by César Aira

A NEW DIRECTIONS
PAPERBOOK ORIGINAL

Originally published in Spanish as *Diez* by Ediciones Ercilla in 1937,
Santiago de Chile. This translation of *Diez* is published by arrangement
with Ampi Margini Literary Agency and with the authorization
of the Fundación Juan Emar.

Manufactured in the United States of America
First published in 2024 as New Directions Paperbook 1604

Library of Congress Cataloging-in-Publication Data
Names: Emar, Juan, 1893–1964, author. | McDowell, Megan, translator.
Title: Ten : stories / Juan Emar ; translated by Megan McDowell.
Other titles: Diez. English
Description: First edition. |
New York : New Directions Publishing Corporation, 2024.
Identifiers: LCCN 2024024864 | ISBN 9780811232074 (paperback) |
ISBN 9780811232081 (ebook)
Subjects: LCSH: Emar, Juan, 1893–1964 — Translations into English. |
LCGFT: Short stories.
Classification: LCC PQ8097.Y2 D5413 2024 | DDC 863/.62 — dc23/eng/20240610
LC record available at https://lccn.loc.gov/2024024864

2 4 6 8 10 9 7 5 3 1

New Directions Books are published for James Laughlin
by New Directions Publishing Corporation
80 Eighth Avenue, New York 10011

Table of contents

On Juan Emar

IN HIS YOUTH, ÁLVARO YÁÑEZ BIANCHI (1893–1964) used the ironic pseudonym of "Juan Emar" (from the French *j'en ai marre*, or "I'm fed up") to sign the combative articles on art that he published between 1923 and 1925 in *La Nación*. The newspaper belonged to his father, Eliodoro Yáñez, a prominent man: he was a senator, Minister of Foreign Affairs, and government advisor. He published *La Nación* between 1917 and 1927. His son, the only surviving boy along with several daughters, spent a good deal of his life in France, first in Paris and later in Cannes. After his adolescence, he spent three stints of a few years in Chile, and that was when he wrote all of his published oeuvre. His first return, when he was thirty years old, lasted only two years. That time, he arrived in February 1923, excited to promote the artistic vanguards of Europe, and along with some artist friends (including Camilo Mori and Luis Vargas Rosas) he created a group, which they named the "Grupo Montparnasse," in order to disseminate the latest artistic currents. In October they presented an exhibition, and from then on Emar's "Notes on Art" appeared in *La Nación*, first biweekly, then weekly. The group's campaign lasted until 1925, when Emar returned to Paris as Secretary of the Chilean Embassy in France, a position he held until 1927 and the only formal occupation he had in his lifetime.

In 1932 he went back to Chile for a second time, summoned by his father, who died that same year. Then, over the next five years, Emar wrote and published all of his visible work. In June of 1935 he self-published three books, two of them short — *Ayer* (Yesterday) and *Un año* (One Year) — and one longer work, *Miltín 1934*. At the same time he was writing those books, he had also written almost all the stories that appeared in 1937 in a volume titled *Diez* (Ten). The books were met with total critical silence and public indifference — quite inexplicably, given the surprising nature of the texts.

Yesterday is the story of one day, from morning to night, which the narrator spends in the company of his wife. The first of the eight short chapters, detailing the morning's first outing, relates the spectacle of the guillotine decapitation of a criminal, Rudecindo Malleco, convicted of a strange crime involving his wife, Matilde Atacama (Emar's characters reappear throughout his stories). From there, the couple heads to the zoo, where they witness a concert of monkeys and the devouring of a lioness by an ostrich. The episodes grow more rarefied as the day passes. The penultimate one involves an odd maneuver with a urine stream at a urinal, which, curiously, recalls Duchamp's famous readymade. (It's likely that Emar was aware of the work, since he had been in contact with the Surrealists in Paris.)

One Year is the diary of a year with only twelve entries, each made on the first day of the month. Very strange things also happen here, starring the characters who will populate all of Emar's work: in the entry from July 1, the "cynic Valdepinos," one of Emar's many alter egos, appears; in October's entry, during an astonishing seaside adventure, we encounter Desiderius Longotoma, another recurring figure.

Miltín 1934, much more extensive and ambitious than the other two books, derives its name from an Araucanian cacique who may have really existed, and was defeated by Pedro de Valdivia. The cacique mourns his defeat, and also, according to legend, mourns in advance for the evils that will beset Chile throughout its history. The through line of the book is the intention, indefinitely delayed, to write a "Midnight Story," until on the final page, midnight of December 31 arrives and the book ends. It is uneven and somewhat tedious, with realistic passages, childish jokes, and long, fairly conventional diatribes against critics of both literature and the visual arts. It is partly redeemed by moments of truly fantastic invention, like the interplanetary voyage on Lorenzo Angol's plane, or a description of prehistoric mosquitoes discovering and studying the eye. (This episode is the only one that justifies Neruda's comparison of Emar to Kafka, because of its similarity to "Investigations of a Dog." But I think the likeness is casual; the two authors' processes and atmospheres are very different. Emar has no precedents, nor equals; echoes and similarities — Lautréamont, Macedonio Fernández, Gombrowicz — have more to do with the inclinations of their readers.)

Miltín 1934 augurs the tendency toward discursiveness that Emar will employ unchecked in his secret work. Begun in 1940 and only interrupted twenty-four years later by Emar's death, this book is an immense novel that takes the form of a door; he eventually wrote the three or four thousand pages of the first part, *Umbral* (Threshold), and a couple thousand of the second, *Dintel* (Transom). Here his visions lose the arbitrariness that gave them their charm, and instead become vehicles for laborious allegories. Emar's slow digestion of his esoteric readings (Ouspensky, de Guaita, Rudolf Steiner, and Papus, among others) displaces his invention, the traces of which become ever weaker and more ancillary. Invention was no longer needed for the guiding principle of Emar's final work, and in any case, he had left his inventiveness well-documented in the splendid display panel that is his story collection *Ten*.

Ten was, with good reason, its author's favorite of his own books. He mentions in a letter that one of the stories ("Pibesa,"* the only story that was republished during Emar's lifetime, in the *Anthology of the Modern Chilean Story*, 1958, edited by María Flora Yáñez),

---

* Here rendered as "Lassette." — Eds.

"isn't half-bad." Written during his years of intense literary production, 1933–1935, the stories are grouped in an intriguing thematic pyramid: four animals, three women, two places, one vice.

These ten stories show all the varieties of Emar's fantasy, in their most perfect manifestation. This extraordinary marriage of hallucination and obsession lacks nothing, not even glimpses of the paralyzing digressions that will later take hold of his writing (cf. immobility in front of the "damned cat's" funnel). This is absurdity via an excess of logic, and there is a previous absurdity in the very writing of the text: it seems as though we were witnessing the invention of the art of narrative, or else an exercise in the process of learning how to write stories the way writers do it, except that every part of the lesson (descriptions, circumstantial details, plots, denouement) strikes out on its own and goes crazy ...

Ten was Emar's last publication. By 1940, when he started writing *Umbral*, he had returned to Europe. His youthful marriage to his cousin Mina Yáñez (with whom he had two children, Carmen and Eliodoro) was followed by a second, to Gabriela Rivadeneyra (three daughters: Marcela, Pilar, and Clara), and a final relationship with Alice de la Martinière, who was French and with whom he lived in Cannes until 1955. Then he returned to Chile for good and lived on a country estate called Quintrilpe, in Temuco, owned by his son Eliodoro. There he spent his time writing his long novel, which he was determined not to publish during his lifetime. He also painted, signing his works with his given name, Álvaro Yáñez. As for his reading, it must be said that his undertakings were not limited to the esoteric realm. He was no stranger to the surrealists and their forerunners (*One Year* includes an episode with *The Songs of Maldoror*), a letter or two evidence solid knowledge of Dostoyevsky's work, and detective novels were a regular pastime.

The writing of *Umbral* continued until Emar's death in April of 1964. His disinterest in publication, or even in people reading his writing, led to great lengths, in which brilliant passages (like a trip through The Three Chimneys bar) alternate with plodding philosophy (a dialogue about Time or Music can easily run on for two or three hundred pages). Much of the material from his earlier books reappears recycled here, like his characters, all of them with peculiar names (though none as endearing as the dog's from *Ten*: Piticuti). In a letter to his daughter Carmen (1960), he says: "I write and write and in that way, by writing, one takes on everything and nothing ... There are characters, many characters: Lorenzo Angol, Romualdo Malvilla, Desiderius Longotoma, Woldemar Lonquimay, Don Irineo Pidinco, Doctor Hualañé, Rosendo Paine, Stramuros (a great composer whose name follows in the tradition of Stradivarius, Stravinsky, Stracciari), Reverend Carbuncle the All-Knowing, the architect Ladislao Casanueva, a great Chinese man named Fa, Rubén de Loa, a magician named Bárulo Tarata, the devil incarnate who is named Palemón de Costamota, an initiate named Florencio Naltagua ..."

Six years after his death in 1971, the Editorial Universitaria republished *Diez* with a short prologue by Pablo Neruda. In 1977, in Argentina, Carlos Lohlé started to publish *Umbral*, but never finished. Interest in Emar was rekindled in the 1990s, and has never entirely subsided. The Directorate of Libraries, Archives, and Museums in Chile (DIBAM) finally published the fifty-five hundred pages of *Umbral*. Then came successive republications of *Un año* (1996), *Miltín 1934* (1977), *Ayer* (1998), and, for the first time collected in a book, Emar's *Notas de Arte* (Notes on Art, 2008). In 2006, a selection of his diaries was published under the title *M[i] v[ida]: diarios (1911–1917)*. There is also an *Essential Anthology* (1994), edited by Pablo Brodsky, who wrote the introduction ("Biography of a work") for the edition of *Umbral*, and the prologue and notes for a short collection of letters, *Cartas a Carmen* (1998).

— CÉSAR AIRA

FOUR ANIMALS

The Green Bird

BACK IN THE YEAR OF 1847, A GROUP OF FRENCH scholars sailed aboard the schooner *La Gosse* to the mouth of the Amazon River. Their goal was to study the flora and fauna of the region, and upon their return present a long and exhaustive paper to the Institut des Hautes Sciences Tropicales de Montpellier.

At the end of that year, the *La Gosse* anchored in Manaus and, in six dugouts carrying six scholars each, the thirty-six scholars — for such was their number — headed upriver.

By mid-1848 we find them in the village of Teffé, and at the start of 1949, setting out on an excursion down the Juruá River. Five months later they have returned to the village, now towing two more dugouts loaded with curious zoological and botanical specimens. Immediately thereafter they continue their expedition down the Marañón, and on January 1, 1850, they stop and set up camp on the shores of that same river, in the village of Tabatinga.

Of those thirty-six scholars, I personally am interested in only one, which does not for an instant imply that I disregard the merits and learning of the other thirty-five. This one is Monsieur le Docteur Guy de la Crotale, fifty-two years old at the time; plump, short, with a great red beard, kindly eyes, and a rhythmic way of speaking.

I am utterly ignorant of Doctor de la Crotale's merits, and of his knowledge I haven't the slightest notion (which does not, of course, deny the existence of either). Regarding his contribution to the famous report presented in 1857 at the Institut de Montpellier, I am absolutely uninformed, and I haven't the slightest idea what his long years of labor in the tropical jungles with the aforementioned scholars entailed. None of which negates the fact that Doctor Guy de la Crotale interests me to the utmost degree. Here are the reasons why:

Monsieur le Docteur Guy de la Crotale was an extremely sentimental man, and his sentiments were focused, above all, on the various birds that populate the skies. Among all these little birds, Monsieur le Docteur felt a marked preference for parrots; once the expedition was settled in Tabatinga, he obtained his colleagues' permission to adopt a specimen, care for it, feed it, and even bring it with him back to his country. One night, while all the parrots of the region were curled up asleep, as is their habit, in the leafy treetops of the sycamores, the doctor left his tent, and — striding among the trunks of birches, crabwoods, dipterocarps and chinaberry trees; trampling maidenhair, damiana, and peyote under his boots; getting tangled up in the stems of lattice moss and periwinkle; his nose smarting from the stench of the manga-puchuy fruit and his ears from the creaking of the purging buckthorn trees — on that hazy moonlit night, the doctor reached the base of the tallest sycamore and climbed stealthily up, and with a well-timed dart of his hand, availed himself of a parrot.

The bird thus captured was completely green save for beneath his beak, where two stripes of bluish-black down adorned him. He was medium-sized, some eighteen centimeters from head to the base of the tail, which extended another twenty centimeters, no more. As this parrot is the center of the story I'm going to tell, I will give a few details on his life and death. Here goes:

He was born on May 5, 1821. That is, at the precise moment when his egg cracked open and he began his life, far, very far away, off on the abandoned island of Santa Elena, the greatest of all Emperors, Napoleon I, was dying.

De la Crotale brought him to France, and from 1857 to 1872 he lived in Montpellier, carefully ministered to by his owner. But in 1872, the good doctor died. The parrot then became the property of the doctor's niece, Mademoiselle Marguerite de la Crotale, who two years later, in 1874, entered into marriage with Captain Henri Silure-Portune de Rascasse. This matrimony was barren for four years, but in the fifth was blessed by the birth of Henri-Guy-Hégésippe-Désiré-Gaston. From the tenderest age, this boy showed artistic inclinations — perhaps he inherited the old doctor's refined sentimentality — and of all the arts, he had an indisputable preference for painting. And so it was that when he arrived in Paris at the age of seventeen — for his father had been assigned to the capital's garrison — Henri-Guy entered the École des Beaux-Arts. After taking a degree in painting, he devoted himself almost exclusively to portraits, but then, keenly influenced by Chardin, he began dabbling in large still lifes that included a few live animals. The house cat, posed amid various foodstuffs and kitchen utensils, went under his brushes; then the dog had his turn; the chickens and canary had theirs; and on August 10, 1906, Henri-Guy sat before a large canvas, his subject atop a mahogany table: two flowerpots with a variety of flowers, a lacquer trunk, a violin, and our parrot. However, the fumes from the paint and the strain of posing began to wear on the bird's health, and so it was that on the 16th of that month he let out a sigh and passed away — at the very instant when the most terrifying of earthquakes battered the city of Valparaíso and brutally punished the city of Santiago de Chile, where today, June 12, 1934, I write in the silence of my library.

The noble parrot of Tabatinga, captured by the sage professor Monsieur le Docteur Guy de la Crotale and dead on the altar of the arts before the painter Henri-Guy Silure-Portune de Rascasse, had lived for eighty-five years, three months, and eleven days.

May he rest in peace.

But he did not rest in peace. Henri-Guy had him tenderly embalmed.

The parrot remained embalmed and mounted on a fine ebony pedestal until the end of 1915, when it was learned the painter had died heroically in the trenches. His mother, widowed seven years earlier, thought to travel to the New World, and before setting sail, she auctioned off much of her furniture and possessions. Among these was the Tabatinga parrot.

It was acquired by old père Serpentaire, who kept a store at number 3 rue Chaptal that sold bric-a-brac, antiques of little value, and taxidermy. And there the parrot remained until 1924 without awakening a glimmer of interest in his personage. But that was the year things would change, and here I'll relate the manner and circumstances by which they did:

In April of that year I arrived in Paris, and, along with various friends from back home, dedicated myself night after night to the most roaring and joyful revelry. Our preferred neighborhood was lower Montmartre. On rue Fontaine, rue Pigalle, boulevard Clichy, or the place Blanche, there was no dance hall nor cabaret that did not count us among its most fervent customers. Our favorite was, without a doubt, the Palermo on the aforementioned rue Fontaine, where, between one jazz band and the next, an Argentine orchestra played tangos that were sticky as caramel.

We would lose our heads at the first notes from the bandoneon, champagne would flow down our gullets, and by the time the first singer — a leathery baritone — broke into song, our excitement verged on madness.

Among all those tangos, there was one for which I had a great predilection. Perhaps the first time I heard it — or better yet, "noticed it"; or even better, "isolated it from the rest" — a new feeling shivered through me, a new psychic element was born within me, and, as it burst open and spread outward — like the parrot breaking its eggshell and stretching its wings amid the great sycamore trees — found, in the languid notes of that tango, the matter in which it could develop, strengthen, and endure. A coincidence, a simultaneity, no doubt about it. And although that new psychic element never did enlighten my conscious mind, as those chords broke out I knew with my entire being, from hair to toes, that they — the chords — were full of vivid meaning for me. Then I would dance holding her — whoever she was — tight, with sensuality and tenderness, and I would feel a vague pity for anyone who was not me, rapt, entangled with her and my tango.

The leathery baritone of the *Palermo* sang:

I have seen a green bird
in rosewater bathing.
And in a crystalline vase
a carnation whose petals are falling.

"I have seen a green bird ..." That was the phrase — hummed at first, then only spoken — that expressed all feeling. I personally used it for everything, and it always fit with admirable precision. My friends in commiseration adopted it too, filling it with anything around that seemed ambiguous. This phrase was also a kind of code word in our nocturnal conspiracies, and it spun out a web of understanding pliant enough to accommodate every possibility.

And so, if one of us had a great piece of news to share, a success, a conquest, a triumph, he would rub his hands together and exclaim with a radiant face, "I have seen a green bird!"

If a concern or unpleasantness were to loom over him, in a low voice, with suspicious eyes and frowning mouth, he would tell us, "I have seen a green bird ..."

And so on. Really, we needed nothing else to understand each other; we could express anything we wanted, sink into the subtlest folds of our souls, without needing to avail ourselves of any other words. And life, expressed in this way, with such compression and abbreviation, took on for us a peculiar facet and formed a second life that ran parallel to the first, sometimes clarifying it, sometimes confusing it, and often caricaturing it with such sharp acuity that not even we ourselves could fully and deeply understand where and how it came about.

And, quite often, especially when I was at home and alone after our carousal, I would be hit by an uncontrollable peal of laughter if I merely said to myself, "I have seen a green bird."

And if at that moment I was looking, for example, at my bed, my hat, or at the rooftops of Paris out the window, and then glanced at the tips of my shoes, the internal tickle of my laughter would rise, and would again cast over all my fellow men a drop of pity, of disdain, even, at the thought of how unhappy they all are, all those who have never even once been able to reduce their existence to a single phrase that includes, encompasses, condenses — even fructifies — everything.

In truth, *I have seen a green bird.*

And in truth, I am chuckling a little right now, and I can remember and understand why one might feel sorry for humanity.

One day in October I went out reveling in Montparnasse. I visited various bars in the evening and boîtes at night, and after a succulent repast I went back home with a dizzy head, a full stomach, and liver and kidneys working at full steam.

The following day, when my friends phoned at seven in the evening to plan our carousing, my nurse told them it would be utterly impossible for me to join them that night.

They made the rounds at all our favorite spots, and, what with all the champagne, dancing, and dining, they were caught unawares by the dawn, and then by a magnificent autumn morning.

Arm in arm, intoning the songs they had heard, hats pulled down over their eyes or ears, they went down rue Blanche and turned down rue Chaptal in search of rue Notre Dame de Lorette, where two of them lived. When they passed before number 3 of the second aforementioned street, père Serpentaire was just opening his little shop, and there in its window, before my friends' astonished eyes, rigid atop its big ebony pedestal, was the green bird of Tabatinga.

One of them cried out, "Men! The green bird!"

And the others, more than surprised, were afraid that this was an alcoholic vision, or the very embodiment of their constant obsession. They repeated in soft voices, "Oh … the green bird …"

A second later, normality returned and they rushed into the store as one, demanding to take immediate possession of the bird. Père Serpentaire asked for eleven francs in exchange, and those good friends, moved to the point of tears by their discovery, paid him double, depositing a sum of twenty-two francs into the confounded man's hands.

Then their minds returned to their absent companion, and they headed for my house in lock step. They rollicked up the stairs, to the outrage of the concierge, then knocked at my door and delivered the relic to me. And all of us, in a chorus, sang:

I have seen a green bird
in rosewater bathing.
And in a crystalline vase
a carnation whose petals are falling.

The parrot of Tabatinga took its place on my worktable, and there, his glass gaze resting upon the portrait of Baudelaire I'd hung on the opposite wall, he kept me company during the four years I remained in Paris.

At the end of 1928 I returned to Chile. Snugly packed in my suitcase, the green bird crossed the Atlantic once again, passed through Buenos Aires and the pampas, climbed the Andes and tumbled down the other side with me, reaching the Mapocho Station on January 7, 1929. Its glass eyes, accustomed to the poet's image, curiously took in the low, dusty patio of my house and then, on my desk, a bust of our hero Arturo Prat.

It spent that whole year in peace, and the following year as well. Then, with a nocturnal cannon shot, the year of our lord 1931 began.

And here a new story begins.

On that very January 1 — in other words (perhaps a superfluous detail, but, in the end, it has come to my mind), 84 years after Doctor Guy de la Crotale's arrival in Tabatinga — my uncle José Pedro came to Santiago from the salt flats of Antofagasta and, as there was a guest room in my house, asked my permission to occupy it.

My uncle José Pedro was a learned man, burnished by labors of the imagination, who considered it his most sacred duty to give advice to the youth in the form of long lectures, especially if one of his nephews numbered among the ranks of said youth. Living in my house struck him as a precious opportunity, because — though I don't know how — news of my constant carousal in Paris had reached his ears. Every day during our lunches and every night after dinner, my uncle, speaking slowly, said horrible things about Parisian nightlife, and admonished me for having spent so many years taking part in it, rather than the Paris of the Sorbonne and its environs.

The night of February 9, sipping coffee in my study, my uncle asked me suddenly, pointing a trembling index finger toward the green bird, "What's with that parrot?"

In a few short words I told him how it had come into my hands after my best friends had a raucous night of fun that I had missed, because the previous day I had ingested enormous quantities of food and various alcohols. My uncle José Pedro pierced me with an austere gaze, and then, turning his eyes to the bird, exclaimed, "Vile creature!"

That was it.

It was the trigger, the cataclysm, the catastrophe. It was the end of his destiny and the start of a complete reversal in mine. It — as I observed with a lightning-quick glance at my wall clock — occurred at 10:02 and 48 seconds on that fatal February 9 of 1931.

"Vile creature!"

As the last echo of the final "-ure" faded away, the parrot spread its wings, flapped them with vertiginous speed, and, with its ebony pedestal still stuck to its feet, took flight and shot across the room like a projectile, smashing into poor uncle José Pedro's skull.

Upon impact — I remember it perfectly — the pedestal swung like a pendulum and its base — which must have been pretty dusty — struck my uncle's big white tie, smudging it. At the same time, the parrot cleaved his bald spot with a violent peck. His forehead cracked, gave way, opened up — and from the crack, just as lava flows, swells, surges, and spills from a volcano, so flowed, swelled, surged, and spilled the thick gray matter of his brain, and several trickles of blood slid over his forehead and down his left temple. Then the silence that had fallen when the bird began its flight was filled by the most horrible shriek of terror, leaving me paralyzed, frozen, petrified, since I had never imagined that any man could ever scream in such a way, much less my good uncle, with his slow and rhythmic speech.

But an instant later, my vigor and my conscience came surging back to me, and I picked up an old copper mortar and lunged toward them, ready to destroy the evil bird with one blow.

Three leaps and I raise the weapon, ready to let it fall upon the creature in the very moment it was about to thrust its beak in a second time. But when it saw me it stopped, turned its eyes toward me, and with a slight movement of its head, it hastened to ask me, "Mr. Juan Emar, could you do me a favor . . . ?"

And I, naturally, replied, "At your service."

Then, seeing I was paralyzed again, the bird dealt its second blow. Another hole in the skull, more gray matter, more trickles of blood and another shriek of horror, though more subdued now, weaker.

I again recover my sangfroid, and with it, a clear understanding of my duty. Up goes my arm and the weapon. But the parrot — again — looks at me and speaks — again, "Mr. Juan Em . . . ?"

And I, so as to finish quickly, "At your ser . . ."

Third strike of the beak. My uncle lost an eye. The parrot used his beak like a dessert spoon to scoop it out and then spit it at my feet.

My elder's eye was perfectly round except at the point opposite the pupil, where it had something like a little tail that immediately brought to mind the agile tadpoles that populate the swamps. From this little tail emerged a very thin scarlet thread that led from the floor up into the empty eye cavity, and that, with the old man's desperate flailing, stretched, contracted, trembled, but did not break; the eye, as if adhered to the floor, did not move. This eye was, I repeat — with the exceptions I've noted — perfectly spherical. It was white, white like a marble ball. I had always imagined that eyes — especially old men's eyes — would be slightly brownish in back. But no: white, white like a marble ball.

Through this white ran graceful, subtle, very fine lacquer veins that, mingling with other, even finer veins of cobalt, formed a wonderful filigree, so marvelous that it seemed to move, to glide atop the damp white surface and, at times, even slip off into the air like an illuminated, airborne spiderweb.

But no. Nothing moved. It was an illusion born of the desire — quite legitimate, it must be said — for so much beauty and grace to grow, take on a life of its own and rise up, to recreate vision and its multiplied forms, or the soul with its astonishing realization.

A third scream brought me back to my duty. Scream? Not so much. A hoarse groan; that is, a groan that was hoarse but sufficient, as I've said, to return me to the path of duty.

A leap, and the mortar whistles in my hand. The parrot turns, looks at me, "Mr. Ju ...?"

And I, hastily, "At your ..."

An instant. I stop. Fourth beak-blow.

This one struck at the top of his nose and ended at its base. That is, sliced it off completely.

My uncle, after this, was turned into an appalling spectacle. At the top of his head, from two craters, boiled the lava of his thoughts; the scarlet thread vibrated in his empty eye socket; and in the triangular hole left in the middle of his face by the loss of his nose, a coagulation of thick blood appeared and disappeared, driven out and back in by his panting breath.

Now there was no more screaming or groaning. His one remaining eye, behind his drooping eyelid, could only shoot me a pleading look. I felt it pierce my heart and flood it with all the tender memories going back to my childhood and tying me to my uncle. Before such sentiments I hesitated no more, and lunged frantically and blindly. As my arm fell, a whisper reached my ears, "Mr . . . ?"

And I heard my lips responding, "At . . ."

Fifth beak-blow. It tore off his chin. The chin rolled down over his chest and his big white tie, cleaning off the dirt from the pedestal and leaving, in its place, a yellowish tooth that stuck there, shining like a topaz. Next thing I knew, the boiling up above had stopped, the coming and going of thick bubbles in the triangular nose hole subsided, the eye thread broke, and the chin hit the floor with the sound of a drumbeat. Then his two thin hands fell limp at his sides and from his sharp nails, pointed inertly toward the floor, fell ten drops of sweat.

There was a low whistle. A death rattle. Silence.

My uncle José Pedro passed away.

The wall clock showed 10:03 and 56 seconds. The scene had lasted 1 minute and 8 seconds.

After this, the green bird remained suspended for an instant, then spread its wings, shook them violently, and rose up. Like a kestrel over its prey, it hovered motionless in the middle of the room, the fluttering of its wings making a clicking sound like drops of rain on ice. And the pedestal, meanwhile, swung in time with the pendulum of my wall clock.

Then the creature flew in a circle and finally landed, or, rather, set its ebony foot on the table, and, turning its glass spheres once again to the bust of Arturo Prat, fixed them there in a still, infinite gaze.

23

It was 10:04 and 19 seconds.

On the morning of February 11, my uncle José Pedro's funeral rites were performed.

As we carried the casket to the hearse, we had to pass by the window of my study. I took advantage of my companions' distraction to glance inside. There was my parrot, motionless, his back to me.

The enormous hatred emanating from my eyes must have weighed on his back feathers, especially if we add to this weight — as I believe we should — that of the words hissed from my lips, "I'll get you for this, foul bird!"

Yes, it must have felt it, because the bird quickly turned its head and winked an eye as it started to open its beak to speak. And since I knew perfectly well the question it was going to ask me, I also — to forestall the pointless query — winked, and gently made a slight grimace of affirmation that, translated into words, would be something like the following: "At your service."

I returned home at lunchtime. Sitting alone at my table, I missed my dear uncle's languid, moralistic chats, and always, day after day, I remember them and send a loving thought toward his grave.

Today, on June 12, 1934, it has been three years, four months, and three days since the noble old man passed on. My life during that time has been, for all who know me, the same as the one I have always led. But for me, it has suffered a radical change.

I am more complacent toward my fellow men, for whenever they require something from me, I bow and tell them, "At your service."

Toward myself I have become more affable, for, facing any task of any sort, I imagine said task as a grande dame standing before me, and then, bowing toward the empty air, I say, "Madame, at your service."

And I see the lady smile and turn to walk slowly away. With the result that no task is ever completed.

But in all else, as I've said, I'm the same: I sleep well, eat with gusto, walk happily through the streets; I chat with friends quite agreeably, I go out carousing some nights, and there is, I am told, a woman who loves me tenderly.

As for the green bird, there it is, motionless and mute. Sometimes, every once in a while, I give it a friendly wave, and in a hushed voice I sing to it:

I have seen a green bird
in rosewater bathing.
And in a crystalline vase
a carnation whose petals are falling.

But the bird doesn't move, or say a word.

The Damned Cat

FEBRUARY 21, 1919, WAS A SPLENDOROUS MORNING. No more and no less: splendorous. At six a.m. I saddled Tinterillo, mounted him, and galloped away from the houses down the long, carob-lined boulevard.

My goal was to reach the Melocotón Hills. To do that, you have to go to the end of the aforementioned boulevard, then take the public road some eight blocks, turn right along a path sheltered by dense myrtle branches, and, finally, cross a large alfalfa field. At the end of the field, you're at the foot of the hills.

Two things above all contributed to the splendor of that morning: 1) the temperature; 2) the rural perfumes.

The first was maintained by the velvety rays of a warm sun. It didn't occur to me — as anyone can easily understand — to bring a thermometer along, so it was impossible to check the exact temperature of that delightful air. All I can say is that the horse's gentle gallop provided the precise temperature that the skin translates as not feeling a millidegree of heat or of cold; that is, a temperature so well-calibrated, so exact, so precise, that, while the horse was galloping gently, temperature disappeared.

Well then, hastening the animal's gallop a bit, I immediately felt a pleasant coolness. And if, making the most of his verve, I spurred him to a full-on gallop, outright cold penetrated to the bone. At the end of the public road I pushed my steed to run as fast as his legs could go, but I stopped him after just thirty meters:

the icy cold of a lonely peak high above the clouds was stabbing into my whole body, and I was nearly frozen stiff.

On the other hand, slowing from gentle gallop to an easy trot, a comforting warmth would flood the lungs. And if from there I slowed to a walk, I was immediately reminded that it was summertime at thirty-two degrees latitude. On the carob-lined boulevard, I thought to stop for a moment. A burst of fire suddenly enveloped me, as if my horse and I had found ourselves in a gigantic oven. And so, aside from these moments of experimentation, I stuck to a measured, gentle gallop, and for most of the ride felt no temperature at all.

As I galloped along, I tried to take as much pleasure as possible in the wide gamut of ice and heat that splendorous morning placed at my disposal. I kept Tinterillo's speed perfectly controlled so that temperature was completely annulled. Then I played the following game: I reached my right hand backward to touch the animal's haunches, and then, with my arm fully extended, I thrust it forward to touch his ears. Naturally, my hand's velocity as it made that gesture was equal to that of the horse's gallop plus its own; that is, by making said gesture more or less swiftly, my hand could reach the speed of a rapid gallop, an all-out gallop, or a sprint. As such, depending on how fast I thrust hand toward ears, I felt the full range of cold in my hand, while the rest of my body felt no noticeable temperature. I can assure you that this was very pleasant, as pleasant as is possible in this world. And that's not all. Once at the ears, my hand made the same movement back toward the hindquarters, so that its speed was its own minus Tinterillo's. Then, according to my hand's greater or lesser velocity, I felt the full range of heat, and when I thrust it backward at the same speed at which the horse was going forward, it was motionless, and I could have easily singed my fingertips.

After entertaining myself with this — I repeat — very pleasant game, I wanted to take it further: to accelerate my movements to the maximum, both forward and backward. Going forward, to double the horse's speed, if possible; going backward, to first reach the point of motionlessness and then go even slower.

I made the first attempt as I entered the myrtle path. The second, midway along said path. The first time, I cried out in pain before I'd even managed to touch the horse's ear with my hand. It was as if a hundred razor blades had cut me; then, total numbness. My hand was green and hard. I gave it a tap with my left hand: it sounded like a billiard ball. Luckily, just as we started down the path, I saw a stone wall rise up on one side. I immediately grabbed a stone and rubbed it hard over my frozen limb. Stones from the top course of walls, as is well known, store away a little heat each summer; if the wall has existed for over seventy years, all you have to do is rub one of its stones until the first layer flakes away, and the heat stored up in the deeper layers can radiate out. And thus I saved my hand.

I did think that if the experience of ice had gone so awry, it would be even worse with fire. Still, when would I see such a morning again? How could I leave things half done? If I *could* experience it, how could I not? I was decided.

Holy hell, the pain! This time I didn't just cry out: I howled. My hand burned as red as a tomato. Happily, as everyone knows, the myrtle produces myrtlines, and the plants there were heavy with the purple berries. I picked one with my left hand and squeezed it hard so its sugary juice would drip onto my combusting hand. Blessed relief! Myrtline juice condenses all the subzero temperatures that the myrtle plant endured during the previous winter, and, since the winter of 1918 had been exceedingly cold — the thermometer dipped below zero fourteen times — the fruit's juice easily brought my hand back to normal.

With no desire to repeat those experiences, I turned to another exercise until I reached the alfalfa field. It was this: While Tinterillo kept up his steady gallop, I moved my right foot forward while I retracted my left, and then I switched, moving my left forward while retracting my right, and so on successively at a measured pace. In this way, when one foot was cooling down to the cold of a mountain peak — which, especially for a few short seconds, is very tolerable — the other heated up to the temperature of a stovetop — which, in similar circumstances, is also very tolerable — while the rest of my body registered these two sensations without feeling a whit of temperature itself. Quite pleasant! Delightful! Better than anything I'd experienced up to then!

And I think that's enough about the temperature of that splendorous morning.

Let us turn to the scents of the countryside.

They were divided into four categories according to the scenery I traversed:

A) Carob-lined boulevard: useful smells;
B) Public road: human smells;
C) Myrtle path: wild smells;
D) Final field: alfalfa smell.

A) Croplands on both sides of the carob-lined boulevard are sown with products that are extremely useful to man. Moreover, there are many lots that feed equally useful animals. Thus, on that road one inhaled something like a compendium of our most urgent needs — a compendium by way of the nostrils.

The first field to the right was sown with wheat. It smelled of bread. Future bread, with a cottony center and crunchy crust; an archetypal bread. Future bread — as I've said — and, as such, all of man's possibilities when it comes to bread.

In the paddock on the other side, several Dutch cows were grazing. They smelled of butter. The same considerations as above: an archetypal butter, because it had not yet been made. That scent entered through the left nostril; the other, through the right. In the sinus they mixed together, and then one lived amid a perfume of bread and butter. But don't forget: all this existed in a primordial reality, and had not yet regressed to material substance. As such: infinite possibilities for a soon-to-be palpable existence.

Next was a vineyard. It smelled of red wine. At first, this scent clashed with the other. But after a few steps the red wine overwhelmed all else, and then, slightly dizzy, one could forgive all his enemies right from the saddle of his horse.

In the next paddock, a hundred hogs rolled in mud. A man, at his ranch near the boulevard, was gutting them. It was surely going to smell like rolled pork, and I was to know all the mysteries latent in the archetype of pigs. But no! When I reached the edge of the pen I could see a wagon driving away in the distance, which I recognized as belonging to the butcher from the neighboring town who bought all the edible parts of this farmer's pigs. This stretch smelled, then, of the useless parts, of putrefaction, of pestilent offal, viscera and excrement. Almost sickening. But the nausea was easy to fight off; I had only to consider that such stuff was not truly pestilent but only useless, and its uselessness made us humans find it pestilent. If someday a use were found, it would become deliciously aromatic.

Then came a field of artichokes that smelled of unfathomable mysteries, since they were already present and flowering and their aroma, on splendorous mornings in the midst of nature, is the scent of destiny. Each artichoke carried the potential of its own destiny, and they all mixed confusingly together. Unfathomable artichoke mystery!

And finally, another paddock with sheep that smelled of wool, of mattresses, of yawns, dozes, and spasms.

B) The public road is lined with rented houses. The tenants of these houses disperse a variety of human perfumes into the road.

I remember the first of these perfumes was that of an elderly man with a graying beard who was stubbornly fuming. The reason for his rage, my olfactory sense could not determine. Then I caught the scent of the momentary submission of a dark, buxom woman around forty or forty-five years of age. I thought, then, that a woman inside that ranch and house had ceded to the old man's furies, but I smelled no more; Tinterillo had already brought me to other doorways.

In front of one of them I smelled a confusing little scent, shapeless and amalgamated. There was something soothing and something violent in it; something that wanted to rise from the ceiling upward, soaring; something else that looked down toward the earth, at the mud, at the trampled bricks. But then it all merged into the crude smell of semen. I thought there might have been a tryst, a fit of love that ended in coitus. Perhaps. My olfactory assessments here were quite vague, since my eyes, unlike on the boulevard, were no help at all.

Further on, I smelled human filth corrupting the soap that had scrubbed it from clothes. The soap's corruption was much more fetid than the filth itself. This latter, to tell the truth, was not entirely unpleasant, no matter what the whole world's academics and every university's professors might claim. In my view, "filth smells bad" is an a priori statement, a mere convention. What's more: I believe that soon, very soon, this matter will be put back on the table, and our ideas about it, newly reexamined and studied, will undergo drastic changes. Naturally, as I passed before that house, the repugnant outweighed the pleasant, but that — I can assure you — was an effect of the soap's decomposition, and also the odorlessness of the clothes. These, in the first instance, had smelled of the factory, of pins, needles and cotton. Then, after they were used, they smelled of summer heat and hardworking laborers in summertime. Then, the conventions of university professors determined that these people, hardworking or not, should yield to the reigning beliefs at universities, academies, and other such places, and judge it necessary to wash said clothing.

And they did. And when they did, there was a moment when the clothes were deprived of the smell of filth and yet still did not smell of dried soap remnants, of the clothesline or the sun or the iron. There was, then, an ambiguous moment, an odorless moment, and I certify and affirm that when an object, whatever it is, that by rights should smell of something, smells instead of nothing, it produces in our olfactory sense a disappointment so sudden that it translates into a smell of unbearable fetidness. That's the truth.

And so true is it, that a little ways on Tinterillo carried me by another door that gave off a whiff of authentic scent, with no mixture whatsoever. The exact smell of our true and hallowed filth. I filled my lungs with it, and I was so absorbed in differentiating and enjoying it down to the very last nuance that I paid no attention to the nature and condition of its human source. Man, woman, old, young? I didn't know. But the vigor and health this whiff impressed upon me gave me the sense — romanticism, youth ...? — that it had to be a brown-haired girl turned dirty blonde by sun, oxygen, and the birds of prey that slice through the air above the roof of her house.

The totality of this smell combined of all the smells of our immense countryside. One could smell its infinite sun-cured desolation, its threshed grain, its living fat, its lunar expansion. And that which concentrated such a varied smell, that which impressed unity upon it, was the human note, a sweaty and consistent note: musk and hoof adapted and merged with the secretions of the irrigated earth and the beasts that eat them.

But Tinterillo was already nearing the final house. That was where I gave his gallop a whirl. Petrified beyond either temperature pole, I passed, then, like a flash of lightning before the door. Still, I managed to smell, almost instantaneously, a scent that was compact, thick, total. I felt a stab of voluptuousness along with a limp abandon. This perfume carried within it sharp lines of warm, hard ice that made my nostrils close, even as the other, total smell, made them flare. I could sense inside the house a scene capable of exuding such a mixture: without a doubt, a man was cleaning from his scythe dense drops of human blood, voluptuous drops, drops to be rubbed all over the length of our bodies, drops to sink our tongues into, drops with slumbering fantasies of total happiness. And as he cleaned them, the steel of the hook squealed the coldness of ether, and the sponge, greased with blood, clawed like ammonia.

But by then we were at the myrtle path.

c) Wild scents.

A hundred kinds of weeds grow among the myrtles, and in these weeds live a hundred kinds of arachnids and insects. This total of two hundred kinds gives off a uniform smell, calm and clumsy. Only three weeds stand out: pimpano, quilehue, and tench fava. Only two animals: the devil's dog and the swamp kissing bug.

Pimpano was scarce there. I caught its scent only twice, and only one of those times did I see its sharp, tobacco-colored leaves. Its scent is like a mixture of boldo leaf, lemon verbena, linden flower, chamomile, borage, lemon balm, verbena, sarsaparilla, fennel, heather, and Andean horsetail, well macerated, filtered, and heated to fifty-five degrees. A welcoming smell, then, which induces an instantaneous reconciliation with all of nature; love for nature in all of its noble aspects and an unbreakable faith that these are much stronger and more enduring than its vile aspects. As such, upon smelling pimpano, one scorns alcohol, opium, morphine, cocaine, hashish, and nicotine, and gives thanks for all the ripe and juicy fruits that fall from trees in that magnificent and holy moment when they abandon their sustainer in order to become sustenance in turn. Oh, blessed and benevolent harmony with all that exists! Nothing to be remedied, nothing to add, nothing to take away. I thought of the Moon, and, stupefied, I remembered with a start that in my life outside the pimpano's aroma, I had often wished for the Moon to appear and show me the landscape in a different light, or keep me company as I cried over some romance . . . What a sinful inversion of roles that wish seemed to me now! Under the pimpano, as I thought of the Moon I only felt — only knew — that when there's a Moon up above, down here one should be asleep. And little by little, drowsiness overcame me, and I was about to fall from the horse, fast asleep. But suddenly I considered the Sun: up there, awake, vigorous! Oh Sun, poor, reviled Sun! Forgive them! They know not what they do! You too are used and abused for a thousand things that are not in your purview. Now, thanks to the pimpano, I know the truth, your truth: I know that when you shine majestically, a man must only wake up, walk, eat, bellow or sing, defecate, fornicate. But he should not look at you, nor at the curious nuances and arabesques that you like to shape in various corners, no! That is also inversion, violation of the sainted order of things as revealed to us by this herb.

The quilehue is very different. It has a smooth, cylindrical trunk of a pale orangish shade with flat, oval, hard leaves speckled with white, blue-striped dots, and its cactus shape gives it a slightly diabolical look. Its smell — well, that is starkly diabolical. A curious thing: though I inhaled several times, deep as could be, I didn't smell a hint, not a one, of sulfur, and so can affirm: the Devil does not smell of sulfur. This is, then, a popular belief that is unfounded. The smell of the quilehue — and, as such, of the Spirit of Darkness — is midway between bedbugs and Socotrine aloe. This smell irritates the mucous membranes in the nostrils, forcing one to squeeze one's entire nose with a handkerchief, hard. Doing this, one feels in the nose a sort of muffled pain, which, after several seconds, takes on a certain resemblance to the taste of sexual ejaculate. If in that moment one removes the handkerchief and deeply inhales the scent of the quilehue, hundreds of violent passions are unleashed within that a moment before were not even suspected. Naturally I will keep quiet about those that assaulted me, though I cherish an unshakable conviction that any of my peers who had the same experience would be astonished at the nest of demonic instincts asleep within them. How far away the life-giving Sun and the sedative Moon seem now! Now I know, I know with the most absolute certainty, that the former's only mission is to cultivate fevers and accelerate putrefactions; the latter's, to put us in touch with ghosts and larvae and to help us violate, with black invocations, all that is considered sacred and venerable. Nothing more. Those who are scandalized or who doubt these statements, well, let them smell some quilehue and then we'll talk.

The tench fava smells of interplanetary distances.

The nostrils flare in such a way that all the myrtles and their entire world rush inside, preceded by the tench fava. Then the entire landscape rushes in. Then the world fits itself in. Then the planets. Meanwhile, the smeller is disconcerted, disturbed, by such a flow of enormities up the nose. But when the last planet has gone in, calm is restored, and one can smell the tench fava, smell its true scent. The tench fava smells of interplanetary distances. It smells of salt. The whole of space, as soon as one moves away from its floating nuclei, smells of salt. The common smell of salt that we all know (not the smell this mixture exudes) is only an approximation of the true salt smell. After catching a whiff of this aroma, I resolved — at the risk of singeing myself as on a stovetop — to halt my mount and prolong my enjoyment of that grandeur, as soon as my olfactory sense indicated the plant was near or my eyes showed it to me in the distance. That moment soon came. There, some hundred and fifty meters away, I glimpsed its limp, serrated leaves tinged a variety of greens. Almost immediately, I felt a little chilly: without realizing it, I had spurred Tinterillo to a gallop. We arrived. We stopped. A tongue of hellfire burned us. But, enduring as long as I could, I inhaled. In came the first cascade, with our first planetary world. Though I was familiar with it, I felt that same stupor once again. Until, as the final distractions of Neptune's aromas sank away behind me, I found myself breathing in the pure salt of the beyond, without yet smelling the emanations of Alpha Centauri. Salt! I could only savor it for a split second, as the scent was abruptly scrambled, mixed, sullied, undone. Confounded by this phenomenon, which I couldn't blame on the presence of some foul-smelling sun, I approached the leaves of the tench fava. What bad luck! A devil's dog had just hopped onto them, and it reeked abominably.

I had seen several of these bugs in insect collections. Once dead, they have no smell at all. They are extremely beautiful, and their beauty is quite singular. Gazing upon a specimen, one murmurs to oneself: "how wonderful!" and also: "how awful!" They are seven to eight centimeters long from the tip of the head to the end of the abdomen — that is, not counting their front legs, which emerge from the neck and are the same length as the rest of the bug's body. Those front legs are thick, lilac-colored, covered with sharp points, and they terminate in maroon claws that are very strong. These are, then, more like hands than feet. The creature almost always holds them up and moves them with startling speed. In the very short time I looked at the insect — its stink was choking me, and then there was the burning heat from my having halted — it scratched itself with the right claw once behind the neck and three times under the thorax; with the left, once on the anus and once on each of its legs proper. It also used both of them to smooth its antennae several times and its wings twice, and, finally, the left claw caught a fly, bursting it open, and the right snatched a bumble bee that was buzzing by, which it raised up and threw no less than ten meters away. Its little head is oval-shaped, with two tiny eyes that are uniquely animated. They blink, wink, doze, shine. Its neck is haughty. Its thorax, small. Its waist, slender. Its abdomen, long and robust. Its clear, fine-nerved wings are of a watery green. Its body is an earthy green, except for the legs, which are scarlet. I can't help but give this description since, although its stench and the heat drove me to make my escape tout de suite, I was, for the instant I looked at it, captivated by its strangeness. I couldn't stop thinking about what an unpleasant guest it would be in our bed-sheets, or imagining what a fright, what a horror it would be were it the size of a calf. But, as I said, the thing stank abominably. It was a stench of living rot, a healthy rot, the rot not of death but rather of the lord and master of life, queen and empress of all that exists. I dug in my spurs, bidding farewell to the infinite realms of salt and of the potential domination of the smell of death in all that teems, thinks, and lives.

The swamp kissing bug is a very different thing. It is big (5 to 6 centimeters long by some 3 or 3.5 centimeters wide), flat, squat, heavy, and hard. It sleeps constantly, buried in swamp mud and quaking grass among the myrtle roots. Its presence is discernible to the eye only because it has a proboscis that pokes up from the quagmire, erect. When entomologists spy one, they dig all around it with their spades and soon pull out a reddish something that squirms and waves six short legs shaped like spatulas. As I've said, they sleep constantly, with one exception: one night per month, when the Moon is in its waning gibbous phase. Then they get hungry. They dig themselves out with their spatulas, and, beating their horned wings, take to the air, buzzing like little airplanes. They look for humans in particular, but if they can't find one, they'll attack any beast. With a speed unsuspected in such seemingly sluggish creatures, they dive at their victim's neck, latch onto it with their six spatulas, and bury their proboscis in the carotid artery to gorge themselves on blood. Then the base of their abdomen, until then flat against the lower part of the back, inflates like a balloon blown up by a child. It swells, turns transparent, and finally gets so big and heavy that the insect's six feet, spatulate or not, can't hold on, and the bug plops down, inert, with a dull, dry sound.

One might wonder why a man attacked in this way failed to take a hundred precautions upon hearing the insect's buzz; or, at least, at first contact, didn't slap himself in the carotid and destroy it. Furthermore: if for some reason or other he couldn't avoid being bitten, how is it possible that afterwards, once the bug has fallen — I repeat, nearly inert — he doesn't stomp it with his foot? Incredible as this may be, that's how it is, and in this land or any other inhabited by the swamp kissing bug no man has ever been recorded killing one after suffering its attack. The reason for this strange fact is the following:

As soon as the swamp kissing bug is within fifteen meters of the man, it produces in him a certain numbing effect that translates not so much into a greater or lesser loss of consciousness, but rather a vague feeling of indifference. Fifteen meters is also the distance at which a good ear will first perceive the insect's buzzing. It's worth noting that opinions diverge slightly here: there are those who believe it's the buzzing itself that produces the effect, and others who say that the bug's mere presence is the cause — that is, buzz or no buzz. Whatever the case, it's true that the latest beliefs tend toward this second hypothesis (that the sound of its flight is inoffensive in and of itself).

I have called the effect of this creepy-crawler's presence a "feeling of indifference." That's incomplete. It could also be called a feeling of apathy or pessimism, maybe even of rebelliousness. I don't know exactly. So, instead of trying to define it with a word, I will try to briefly describe its various phases.

When the man senses the enemy's presence — I prefer to say "sense" rather than "hear," though the two are almost simultaneous — that is, when the bug is some fifteen meters away, he says to himself more or less the following:

"A swamp kissing bug? It's still a ways away. No point taking precautions now. There will be time for that. If it latches onto my carotid — then it'll suffer! Well now. What were we thinking about?..."

And the good man goes on thinking about whatever was occupying him at that moment. The bug comes and grabs hold of his neck with its six feet. The man thinks, "A swamp kissing bug . . . I should kill it when it bites my carotid. When it bites my carotid, I will kill it. But now . . . Now, raising a hand, hitting it, interrupting all my thoughts, delaying their conclusion because of the bug with its six little feet . . . And my thoughts are grand, so grand!"

And the good man goes on with the matter occupying him. The bug perforates his carotid with its proboscis and sucks. The man thinks, "A swamp kissing bug . . . It's sucking a little blood. And this night is beautiful and vast. Such a beautiful night, while frightening crimes and backwards cruelties lash the whole world. And meanwhile, limitless hopes arise everywhere. Poor swamp kissing bug! Our bad luck is not its fault!"

And the good man returns to the matters occupying him. The bug balloons. Already, beneath its carapace, it's a cherry of blood. The man thinks, "Well! Tomorrow is another day! The Moon's sweet snores prove it. And these fields, and the evils . . . It's my own fault for concerning myself with them, with those nonexistent evils, for having forgotten about the Moon and its fields. Kill it? If everything — understand, everything! — is evil, then, why execute a swamp kissing bug? Some solution! And not everything can be bad. If it were, I as a man would have known it, and would have dealt the blow!"

And the good man tries to return to the matter at hand. The bug can't take anymore. Its six feet are powerless to hold up its body, now practically a purple plum hanging down. It lets go. It bounces off its victim's shoulder. It falls. And it hits the ground with a dry and dull sound. The good man turns around, looks at it, and thinks, "A swamp kissing bug . . . If there really were so much evil, the whole world would have already exploded. And it hasn't! Proof: nothing around me is exploding. Everything is peaceful and still. The Moon. Crushing you with my foot would only confirm my fear of the evil you could do me. Stay there! It's not for me to correct all of existence with such a small thing. Well! Tomorrow will be another day! Maybe."

And the good man goes on with his walk, forgetting, totally forgetting the matter that had occupied him, barely conserving a nebulous notion that there had even been a moment when he had, in fact, been occupied. The swamp kissing bug wallows sluggishly and has completely idiotic nightmares. But no sooner does the first drop of light fall through the air than it can again beat its horned wings, rise up a little ways and fly very slowly toward its swamp, with the sound of an obese geezer dozing and belching. And the man spends his whole life, up to his last minute, wavering between evil and good, but partly, ever so halfheartedly convinced that no matter what the case may be, it is not his responsibility to settle the question anyway. When they see him, old ladies point at him with the nail of their index fingers and murmur, "Careful with that one! He's surely been bitten by a swamp kissing bug."

But let's move past this parenthesis and back to the matter at hand.

The insect reburies itself entirely, except for its proboscis, which it uses to breathe. It breathes at two different speeds: one extremely slow inhalation, and an exhalation that is comparatively very fast. The former takes up all the days and all the nights between one gibbous moon and the next, less twenty-four hours. The aforementioned period's final twenty-four hours are used to expel the air that was inhaled so unhurriedly during the entire preceding month. Now, while the creature is inhaling, it does not give off a smell — that's when entomologists have to make use of their eyes and their spades. But when the bug exhales — that is, during the twenty-four hours preceding the gibbous phase — it smells, its smell extends widely, its odor rises to such heights that it can be placed alongside all those I have mentioned so far. I deduce from this, as such, that the morning of February 21, 1919, preceded a gibbous phase of the Moon. That morning, the swamp kissing bugs smelled.

Their smell is dull, slow, overpowering. It smells a lot like the torture that Tierra del Fuego natives inflicted on their enemies back in the fourteenth century: they placed an iron circle around the skull and tightened it by turning a screw very slowly. A smell of desperation and anguish. A totally hollow smell. At first it gives rise to a feeling of disgust, but then one sees that feeling any sort of disgust would be pointless. What for? Above all, the nausea is impossible to fix in place, to retain, for as soon as it emerges it dissolves into the hollow of that smell. Once the disgust is diluted, and one has been subjected through the nose to the most absolute vagueness and vacuity, he can perceive off in the distance, in a place that is flat like a platform, a persistent hint of aged blood. Vain is the desire to figure out whether it originates in our own nostrils, in the swamp kissing bug, or in the air itself. Reason would have us believe that the smell emanates from the bug and wafts into our nose, but our soul's entire feeling contradicts that idea, assuring us that not only does the smell permeate the atmosphere, but the whole of the atmosphere is not and can never be anything but that diluted and aimless aroma that drives one to utter curses with the most perfect serenity. In any case, when the insect's emanations filled me, it occurred to me that there is not and has never been a single reason for Columbus to have sailed the high seas just to discover continents so overly vast.

But Tinterillo was galloping, and his gallop reached the end of the myrtle path. I lowered a gate and breathed in the sun. Before me, a large and violet alfalfa field. Gallop!

D) Smell of alfalfa.

Everyone knows, I think, how alfalfa smells, at least everyone in the country of Chile. A healthy and optimistic smell. A soft, prudent smell. A smell that grants our minds the freedom to consider and judge this life and all others as they wish, but that sweetly inclines them toward the conclusion that each life holds within it a justification for goodness.

For me, alfalfa has one other meaning. It incites me to pick its flower, put it in my mouth, and chew. It incites me, once I've chewed it, to dip the tip of my tongue in its juice, and, once tongue has touched juice, to give myself up to the recollection of my life's most pleasant moments. That morning, that's just what I did. I pulled off a handful of flowers, and, squeezing them tight in my hand, I let the horse cross the field as I began to anticipate the intense pleasure of remembrance I was about to have.

My fingers full of flowers, I reached the foot of the Melocotón Hills. Two massifs sloped like the backs of whales to either side. In front of me, gentle peaks rose up into the violet blue. I halted Tintorillo and sniffed.

Not a smell. Nothing but air, air and air. A bit of hill smell . . . perhaps. But above all, air. No peculiarities about the temperature, not a single one. Whether I stood motionless, or moved or ran — nothing! A warm summer morning planted in our immense fields. Peace.

I chewed the alfalfa flower, squeezing out its juice. My tongue, keen as a snake's, darted. And I was able to evoke my past happiness.

On to that!

Two years prior to that morning, in the neighboring city of San Agustín de Tango, a great old friend of mine had ceased to exist: Fa, a Chinese man. He was the happy and peaceful owner of a junk shop near the Santa Barbara river. Whenever my errands or family duties brought me to that city, I made a point of stopping by and seeing him every day, if only for a moment, and we'd chat amiably for several minutes. In addition to his small business, this good man possessed a mysterious secret that, as he told it, a nomadic tribe had revealed to him a few years before the Great War, on one of his many trips through the Gobi desert. Fa, then, in his life of wandering, had learned how to make candiyugo.

He went on making it here in Chile for his own personal use and for a few friends, among whom I had the honor — no, the pleasure — of being counted. He sold each little stick of candiyugo for a hundred and forty pesos, a laughable sum given the pleasures it afforded, even if it seems exorbitant at first.

The stick of candiyugo is — or rather was — cylindrical, two and a half centimeters long by seven millimeters in diameter, and of a smoked almond color. My good friend would never tell me how it was made nor the proportions of its various ingredients. Only once did he venture to say what those ingredients were, but how to manipulate them, how to measure them out — he never confided that. He took his secret to the grave, which is why, on that morning two years ago, its joy no longer existed for me, nor did I have any hope that it would ever exist again.

When Fa's tongue loosened for a moment I hurried to write the ingredients down, thinking perhaps he'd get it into his head to fill in the recipe's details some other time. And maybe my good Chinese friend even had plans to do so. But one day death came for him, and that was the end of the story. Anyway . . .

Candiyugo was composed of thirteen elements, namely: Arabian cinnamon, angelica root, nutmeg, sweet flag, bone marrow, mountain hops, great cardamom, scale of bream, liver of stone curlew, antennae of mole cricket, eye of lamprey, wild boar lips, and Taka-Diastase. That's all I know.

The method of administration was very simple: find a solitary place and a comfortable position. Then hold the little stick with your incisors so that most of its length is inside your mouth. Next, palpate it with the tip of the tongue, with a very slow, circling movement. And then: supreme joy, supreme joy that lasted as long as it took the candiyugo to dissolve — that is, four minutes.

I wouldn't know exactly how to define what this unparalleled happiness consisted of. Perhaps like this: all of one's senses went to sleep except for taste, which situated itself in every part of the tongue's surface that came into contact with the candiyugo. And now, with all the senses completely asleep, the tongue's sensitivity was heightened to a degree that would be unimaginable to any man — imaginative as he may be — who hadn't tried the substance. And this sensitivity soon took on a very odd peculiarity: it was not just sensitivity of taste, but also, to a certain extent, a differentiated sensitivity of all the senses. It was something like seeing with the tongue, hearing with the tongue, smelling and touching with it, and of course also tasting. The brain formed an image of the world, of all reality, that was totally different from the one the senses effect in their normal state. This produced a sense of sight, of hearing, of smell and taste so vastly different that one's comprehension of reality shifted, and the degree of one's daily self-deception (the result of judging by the senses) became so clear that one might say to oneself: "Oh, right! Now I get it! Now I understand, now I know the origins of man's errors and his inability to form a stable conception that would put him in accord with reality. Now, yes!" And the tongue went on showing you — as if it were eyes, ears, nostrils, fingers, and the tongue itself — a sort of counterpart of what is normally shown by those organs; it went on, while all the ingredients of the candiyugo melted and ran through your mouth, all except for one, except for the great cardamom. But, in the last five seconds of the fourth minute, the tongue has probed that ingredient too. The great cardamom dilutes, and, as it dilutes, the five new senses meld into one, just one, their differentiation ceases and a single sense is created, or rather, a single sense that is seeing, hearing, smelling, touching, and tasting simultaneously with a single organ; and then one understands not just reality, not just its relationship to us and to our comprehension, but also, and above all, the original cause that gave rise to it.

But the great cardamom has run out in turn. The tongue comes to a stop and is tongue once more, a tongue that, pressing against the palate, still tastes for a few seconds longer a remembrance of candiyugo in its entirety, which disperses down the gullet and through the whole body an imponderable something that has a subtle kinship with the juices of the alfalfa flower.

This passes in turn. Eyes open, ears hear, nose smells, fingers touch. Reality is divided into five, and one returns to the state of not understanding anything and asking a furious, desperate, annihilating "what for?"

But deep down, the memory of having once known what is and what for remains. Then one looks upon people and their doings, upon stars and their orbits, upon God and his notions with more serenity. And one blesses Fa for having had the good idea to go off into the Gobi Desert, and several personages of that nomadic tribe for having had the even better idea of revealing to my poor and generous friend the secrets of how to make candiyugo.

But all of that is the past, the remote past.

That morning, like so many others over the course of the two years following the death of my good Chinese friend, I did the next best thing: I tasted the juice of my flowers. In this way, I relived the little stick's final moment. As I did, a distant echo of the twelve substances and the great cardamom resonated inside me. A distant echo, yes, very distant ... But in any case it was an outright joy to be able to approach — though, I repeat, from a great distance — those magnificent moments.

And that's how it was on that morning, at the foot of the Melocotón Hills, when I evoked my lost happiness.

A moment later I began to explore the broad hills with my eyes. Three ravines snaked around and disappeared into their gorges. I was most tempted to delve into the one right in front of me, because there, at its entrance, it was bristling with tall trees. But some silly, utterly baseless rationale made me immediately conclude that if this ravine had tall trees at its entrance, it must have very small and stunted ones at the end, and I went on to deduce that the ravine with the feeblest trees at the outset must be adorned at the end with the most towering and leafy ones. An absurd idea that could have no logical basis, I agree, but I thought it and believed it. As such, without a second's hesitation, I turned to the left-hand ravine and headed into it.

For a long time I advanced at the labored pace of my horse, who had to constantly dodge rocks and bushes, searching for — or rather improvising — some kind of a path. Needless to say, the reasoning that led me to choose this ravine over the others turned out to be utterly wrong. The trees were not getting larger at all; there were some tall ones here and there, but most were average size, like all common trees. And so, after an hour of riding, I felt a bit cheated. I stopped, then, and dismounted, and I left Tinterillo to graze in peace while I smoked with my feet on the ground.

Then I went a little further on foot. Underbrush, some shrubs, a trickle of water over the pebbles, and nothing more.

A heavenly peace prevailed. As though to emphasize that peace, every once in a while an Andean buzzard flew overhead, very high up, its wings outspread and motionless. Then it would disappear behind a peak, and stillness settled in again over the muffled silence of the hills. Then, for brief instants, this silence was broken: hidden among the underbrush, a spotted hen bird sang. How beautiful is the spotted hen bird's song! It's a firework, a snaking flame that stretches through the dark sky and pauses at the horizon, booming like a cannon, and then scatters into a thousand tongues of fire and a thousand sparks, whistling the way poppies and chrysanthemums whistle. That's how the spotted hen bird sings. And while it sings, in the dizzying heights above, calm, slow, in black silence, another Andean buzzard soars. What a truly splendorous morning!

I kept going.

With delight, in the warm half-light of the gorge, I suddenly saw a stand of leafy trees whose tops were illuminated by the sun, surely filtered through some mountain canyon. I reached them. With even greater delight I confirmed that they were hiding another surprise, for as soon as I stood beneath their branches I saw, some hundred fifty meters away, an enormous rock. I have always been crazy about rocks, especially ones that rise up alone in the dry hills amid a thousand weeds and twisted shrubs. I walked toward it with long strides, intending to circle it and catch out among its cracks some comfortable seat that would later serve me as a regular site for future reading. What a lovely way to read! In all of nature, rocks are the only things that can rival man's industry in terms of comfort — for sitting, you understand. And then, between one line and the next, to gaze up at the immense Andean buzzards, to hear the lonely crystal song of the occasional spotted hen bird. I began, then, to circle my rock by turning to my left, that is, counterclockwise. I don't know why I include that detail; it came to my pen of its own accord. But I had scarcely circled a quarter of it when I realized that the rock, just like the stand of trees a moment earlier, was there to hide and then reveal another surprise. But while the first one was enchanting, this one was curious, piercingly curious. For here is what appeared before my eyes:

A little more than a hundred meters away, in front of me and at a right angle to the gorge as a whole, there yawned, at ground level in the mountain's flank, a perfectly circular tunnel of about three meters in diameter. From where I stood, it was black, black, which helped to spur my curiosity, so without further ado I ran toward the threshold of that unexpected cave. I reached it, stopped, sat on a stone I found there, and looked inside.

This cave, gallery, or tunnel — call it whatever you like — had the following particularities: its diameter at the entrance was exactly 2.70 meters, so clearly my first calculation, though done from 100 meters away, was fairly accurate. It was straight but progressively shrank in diameter, so that it formed a sort of horizontal funnel. The length of this funnel was 11 meters, at the end of which its diameter was 50 centimeters. At this point a sort of niche opened up, which was, naturally, 50 centimeters from top to bottom and side to side, and was 39 centimeters deep. That sums up the dimensions. Now, as for the nature of this tunnel-funnel, I will say that it was all made of dirt — not a pebble in sight — but this dirt seemed extremely clayey and was unquestionably pretty wet. Its color, a fairly grayish brick red. Its texture, more smooth than rough.

Well then, sitting on the rock at the threshold, I looked inside, toward the depths, toward that niche I've just mentioned, and I fixed my eyes, my awareness, my full attention, on the object that was inside it. All the rest — dimensions, shape, color, etc. — I noted instantaneously and automatically without needing even a tenth of a second. I can, as such, say, without falling short of the truth, that when I reached the threshold after my headlong run and sat down on the stone, I was looking at nothing else but the object in question inside the niche.

This object was a cat. A simple, everyday cat, white with a few yellowish spots. It was sitting in profile but its head was turned toward the funnel's entrance — that is, toward me. On said head, between its two ears, there was a flea, a tiny flea no different from the thousands of fleas we have all seen and suffered. That was all. Not much, to be sure. But simple things are very often complicated, so let us establish again, to really implant the scene, the three main points in the funnel: me, cat, flea.

Now then, since the diameter of the circle made by the funnel's entrance was 2.70 meters, and that of the circle at the back was 50 centimeters, the lower point of this latter — where the cat was — was 1.10 meters higher than the lowest point of the former, that is, the point where I was sitting. The cat, on the other hand, measured 28 centimeters from its seat — 1.10 meters high at the base — to its eyes — which, I should say right now so I don't forget it later, were a brilliant green. These 28 centimeters, added to the first height, make a total elevation of 1.38 meters with respect to the threshold of the entrance, that is, the base of my seat. This, in reference to the back of the cave — let us call it "the cat's domain," just to elevate our style. As for the entryway — "my domain" — the stone acting as my seat measured 72 centimeters, and I, comfortably seated and leaning forward a little, measure, from seat to eyes, 66 centimeters. Seventy-two plus 66 equals 1.38. That is, our eyes were at exactly the same height, so it was almost as though, in order to look at each other, we had to launch a visual ray parallel to needle-level; it seems to me, has always, and will always seem to me, that such a ray — even if it is no shorter or straighter than any other, and even if it is more curved than the ideal line, etc. etc. — such a ray is and will always be, to my mind, more fixed, more piercing, stronger, a thousand times stronger, for the very fact that it runs parallel to the earth, parallel to it in spite of and aside from the earth's little hills and depressions, parallel to this earth which is where we are, yes, where we live and suffer, whatever anyone says or thinks.

Regarding our other senses, I have nothing to say. Neither hearing, nor touch, smell, or taste played any role at all, at least not of any importance, in our lives from then onward. If they indeed remained intact and alive, their activities shrank to their most minimal expression — one point less and they would have been entirely suspended. As for the rest of our organisms — mine, in any case, and I suppose also the cat's and the flea's — they began a totally vegetative life. Thus, the sense of sight, and in sight, the ray from eye to eye, became for our existences — that is, for our essence, our meaning, or better yet our reason for being — the vehicle of expression on one hand, and of absorption on the other.

But that's not all. Because really, a ray, a single one, just "one," as I say, is a unit, and as far as I know, it has not as yet been possible to realize any expression of manifested life in the unit one, nor to receive an echo of it, nor generate propulsion, nor maintain balance. Unity, they say, is beyond our world; even though it's the beginning of everything — so they also say — it is inconceivable to us, and so, in my particular case, facing the cat, completely useless.

Oh! But here the flea comes into play! And now, bringing this flea into our system, we will form an organized figure that, because it is a shape and no longer a single unit — which as such could only be unfigurative — can now come to have or be in a relationship, a connection, an affinity, a polarization, if you like, with all the rest of creation, with the other and total figure.

Recall that I said the flea was at the apex of the cat's head; that is, a bit above its eyes, which is to say above the endpoint of my visual ray. Hence, joining this point with the flea by means of another ray — imaginary, to be sure, I know that's how you were going to refute the possible existence of my figure. But my visual ray, is it any more real? Can it be touched, appreciated in any way, or even seen? And yet it exists, it has to exist since I see the cat and he sees me, and, as the two of us — two distant points — see each other, as we connect, something, clearly, has to exist between the two aforementioned points, since otherwise, otherwise ... a moment's thought is all it takes to understand that the cat and I would no longer be what each is to the other. And we are very far (I should say!) from not being what we are to each other. We are, and so much so that I'm afraid we are nothing else, just this ray in question and nothing else.

So, then, joining this end point of the expression of my life, that point there on ... Just where it is physically located, I cannot know and have no reason to. On the cat's forehead, between its two eyes, both places at the same time ... I don't know, and, I repeat, there's no reason to know, because my figure — supported, naturally, at points (that is, the three of us) that are perceptible to physics — is located and constructed alongside, as a mirror image, yes, as a mirror of all that physics records. The point exists, though it cannot be located exactly because there are two of my eyes and two of the cat's, and that's enough. Every time we look another being in the eyes and we see and sense each other, it's the same. Where do we look, and where are we looked at? Where does the gaze land, and where do we receive it? At one point, it can't be more than one, though four eyes are in play. Well then, that fixed point is one support for my figure, and from there I throw upward the new line whose existence cannot be refuted, since otherwise, as I have said, if it did not exist, we'd be right back where we were before, that is, the cat's eyes and the flea would not be what the one is to the other, and vice versa. And they are. Oh, how they are! There they are, there I see them: the cat, the good yellow and white cat, and atop it the annoying flea that bites and bites and naps a while.

As such, we are already united, the three of us connected, me, the cat, the flea, and we form an angle. These are the lines along which our lives pass.

Pass? Not yet! Because as they passed along the lines, they would leave, they would leave forever, they would vanish into the infinite. For the figure has not yet been closed, and, not closed, two doors are left at each of its ends, two mouths open to the infinite nothing. And life must be closed, enclosed, limited, drawn. Otherwise, the entire world, the cosmos, would converge toward the magnet of these two lines, and one half would spray out from the flea's end, and the other from my endpoint that way. And nothing would subsist in anything.

I drew, then, the third line. It started from the flea and came toward me. The two dangerous mouths were closed; the figure of a long, thin, very acute triangle was defined. All of nature — and, I am sure, men as well — paused in admiration, stupefaction, for a hundredth of a second, and then, with the three points now riveted on me, the cat, and the flea, or "on me," "on him," and "on it," as we could now say, as well as "on it," "on me" and "on him"; then life could not only arrive, not only pass, but also circulate, circulate like this: me, him, it; him, it, me; it, me, him ... circulate, circulate always, circulate definitively, alongside, as a mirror image of the other, in miniature, yes, very small, but tightly condensed, compressed and retained; life could circulate there through the long and very narrow triangle finally established and fixed inside the funnel that became its protective casing.

Noon, noon on the dot.

Our composition was finished, established and fixed. And the three of us were established and fixed ourselves.

I was flooded with a very pleasant feeling of repose; more than repose, of stability. I don't know if all living beings have had such a feeling. In any case, I can assure you that for my part, unbeknownst to me, my notion of stability up to that moment had been an abstract and purely intellectual notion, and had never penetrated my organism fiber by fiber as it did then. It changed from a notion, I repeat, to a physical sensation, and this sensation not only took over my body but was also prolonged by the triangle's vibrations, and it encompassed, enveloped, my two silent companions.

I had not the slightest doubt that as the three of us came together that way, we had formed a figure, or, better yet, a stable image — and let's see if I'm doing justice to the feeling we experienced. We had achieved a balance, a perfect balance among discrete forces, loose forces, three different forces that until that moment had been roaming around the world, disoriented and willy-nilly, three incoherent forces in the chaos of life, which, in their very incoherence, their very imbalance, contributed to the steady increase of that chaos, errant as they were. Three forces — desperate in their useless roaming, bitter in their nonemployment, furious in their coerced running, fearful of reflecting their misfortune onto other, already extant forces — were now, in spite of it all, cradled in a balance that could ultimately break, especially if, free and capricious, they themselves, the wind, or ennui drove them against that balance, striking it.

Three forces, picture them, like this: long, very long, so extended in space that, having already ploughed through the all, they had lost their initial shape (long snakes uncoiling), and then, shapeless, took on the shape of being and nothing more; and so far away in time, so remote, that their origins could only have been three paltry, infinitely paltry gestures that the All-Powerful, Omnipresent, and All-Knowing made carelessly when He had the urge to create a world — He thought — of exact equilibrium.

Three forces, like this, picture them — humans! comrades living in ignorance of the danger that could befall you at any moment and annihilate you! — three such forces, humans, which — from one moment to the next, in any random slip-up, in a momentary, imperceptible coalescence at an infinitely small point of collision, unavoidable for us in our great impotence — could drag into imbalance what has been precariously balanced since the day of creation, and, thus destabilizing, could return all things to the very first nothing.

But these three forces had until that morning managed no more than to slide around the cosmos without breaking through, now here, now there, now yonder; the one, sliding around until incorporating into its frenetic sliding the sweet cat that had snored one night beside a stove; another, the flea that leapt from wormeaten wood onto the cat's head; the third, me, yes, my friends! me, who lived in such pleasant peace, smoking, dreaming, paging through old books; me, my life all quiet and good; me, who on that fatal morning had had the idea, without knowing why, to saddle up Tinterillo and head out to gallop down boulevards, roads, and pathways toward the Melocotón Hills.

It will be remarked that everything I have written is the fruit of my own great exaggeration. Even supposing that three disparate forces (for a moment and from an infinite number of combined circumstances) managed to come and manifest there, through the three of us, in the funnel; even then, practically speaking, in life as it is organized and governed, there would be no means, no possibility whatsoever, to produce or arrive at any kind of event because of the very insignificance of their vehicles in that moment: a cat, a flea, and me. It will be argued that, even supposing the formation of perfect balance inside the figure; even supposing that that "inside" became a reflection, a counterweight hung, as I've said, against the mirror of the other, larger equilibrium in which we live and the stars turn; supposing even further, namely that, silent and still, we were — because of the heap of circumstances and mysterious combinations rushing helter-skelter through the ages ever since creation — we were like a microcosm before — no, I'd rather say beside — beside the vast macrocosm; and even supposing, finally — a supposition no man at all versed in the sciences could avoid — that, given an equilibrium, its rupture can, must produce an upset, must liberate forces whose potency, and as such whose consequences, could be incalculable, and, very certainly, disastrous. Even admitting all of that, someone will always argue that in my case (with all suppositions accepted), I repeat, in this tiny little case of mine, all this could be made and unmade hundreds of times without the slightest disturbance of a leaf on the nearby bush or a grain of the funnel's clay. As it broke up, the equilibrium would discharge forces — immense as the three original forces of this equilibrium may have been — as utterly minuscule as those of any of the world's cats, as the cat in question, as my cat, which represents the exact average of the three of us: it is greater than the flea, and, ultimately, less than me. So — such an argument would continue (though the truth is otherwise) — as formidable, gigantic, and immeasurable as everything there in the funnel may have been, by the laws of things, the forces unleashed by the breaking of the equilibrium could only be expressed by means of the three of us, who, if you add up our potential power and divide it into three, possess all the potentiality of three cats in the vastness of the universe. As such, what is there to fear? Why should we remain so static in a ravine lost in those solitary hills?

OK. Such an argument, plain and simple, only flaunts an inconceivable superficiality. Pay attention now.

Three cats. Imagine three cats, and consider the physical strength of three cats as such. Insignificant, certainly. Three elephants, three mastodons, also insignificant. Now, three cats ... It goes without saying! But you're forgetting something, something essential: that here, in my case, we must not consider them as such — as cats — but rather as constitutive forces and above all as elemental in nature — that's it, as elements! I speak of "three cats" because a cat represents the average of the forces in the funnel, even if there was really only one cat, with the other two forces represented by the flea and by me. Hence the figure, the very fine triangle, is drawn and becomes, isolated as we were, a whole, and each part an element in that whole. Hence, we had gone from being free and alive as entities, from being errant and unused as forces, to being three stable elements in a new form that had not existed as such until that moment at twelve noon on February 21, 1919.

From that moment on there was something else in the Universe, an additional formation, a reflection, a mirror. But here, listen well, the word "mirror" could lead one to error. I use it because there in the funnel an other was reflected, the All. But not only was it reflected, it was also reproduced. Let me be clear: it was replicated. It was a new whole, balanced exactly the same as the great whole. Small, negligible, stunted, miserable ... call it whatever you like! But it was a whole. It *was* again; it was two where before there had been only one. The whole had fallen onto the whole and from then on it lived not off of the life of the other, but a life equal to the other's. Don't forget that when the first ray was launched —

from me to the cat — nothing happened there or anywhere else, because the single line was an unexpressed and inexpressible unity. But when the second ray was launched — from the cat to the flea — there were two, and life was manifest. And also remember that when only these two existed, there was a sort of mouth at either end — from the flea outwards, from me inwards — a sort of cut artery that bled. As such, during that moment, that is, before launching the third ray, life, even as it manifested, circulated more than anything. That is, when circulating, it was still the life of the whole; vitalized, yes, but part of the whole. The individuation had not yet occurred, the separation, the reproductive mirror, the new whole beside the whole, the new cosmos beside the cosmos.

The third line was drawn. Remember: it led from the flea to me. We broke off, separate, outside, mirror, but alone, with our own world, our beginnings, our wait for the end.

Twelve! The Universe, everything, I repeat, stopped for the tiniest instant. Then it went on turning. And we, together, also turned.

Out there, orbits and miseries.

Here, silence! Me, him, it ... It, me, him ... Him, it, me ...

Perhaps infinitely.

Twelve!

I had a clear notion of this sudden and momentary halt. Then, as I said, came that very pleasant sensation of repose. But between the two — I'll say now — between that notion and this sensation, other, very different feelings filled me. Between the two I first had a feeling of stupor, or perhaps it's better to say of solemnity and farewell. Then I was pricked by a sudden regret. Then, a feeling of terror as intense as it was short-lived. Only then, once the world had ceased its pause and started functioning once again, and when in turn the funnel with my two companions started functioning, only then was I inundated by that sense of repose I've mentioned.

Let us go through them, then, in order.

A feeling of stupor; somewhat solemn, a goodbye. Because my significance as a man suddenly ended; my sign changed, my "man" sign vanished and was replaced with the sign of an elemental being. I was now designated or connoted by the sign "element." The man, in the sense of the word, in the sense of a being who lives out his life on this earth, the man in me ceased, and I saw all the men who people the world today, all who have peopled it, perhaps all those gestating to people it in the future, I saw all of them move away, I saw them sidestep me in space so they could go right on stomping around the earth, and I could find myself instantly amalgamated, sucked into a different structure and another destiny.

When I used to pass among the crowd in the streets, I would suddenly imagine something like a giant crane whose base was an unimaginable distance away, and whose arm tilted down toward me. Then I pictured myself caught up by one of its pulleys and lifted dizzyingly through the air. I felt certain that I would soon cease to perceive my own motion as it was transferred to the planet from which I was being removed. Then I would see the Earth detach and fall below my feet, drawing an immense circle around them before dwindling, a great sphere at first, a little ball later, shrinking to a point that, now motionless, would lodge itself into a spot in space, and that winking spark would be all I had left of the healthy, warm suns I used to enjoy while strolling distractedly through its streets. And inevitably, as these thoughts set off a solemn feeling of having separated from my lands and my atmosphere, a desperate anguish permeated me, a sharp regret, an unforgivable mistake: all the tasks, all the things I'd left undone! Everything I didn't finish, everything I left open, like a bleeding wound yet to scar over! Every item, every little item — negligible as it may have been — abandoned without its objective roundly completed, would appear, I knew, as I elbowed my way down the street, as a site of decay, an ulcer — it could be as small as you like — that would upset and mortify more than one person, perhaps twisting their destiny, and that person or those people would reproach me for leaving without first having settled or cauterized those miasmatic focal points I had left behind. And those people wouldn't know how much I'd be suffering up there, alone, lost, gazing at the luminous Earth in the heavens below me. Then — always striding through the streets — I'd see how many idle gaps, how much indifferent, feeble procrastination I'd spent my life on, instead of rushing to fill those gaps, instead of seizing my bouts of procrastination, seizing the future dates where they fell and dragging them, still rushing, to the present moment and — cover! scar, cauterize, round off! — all just in case, just in case the crane came — who knows! — in case it came and took me away, so I could be at peace forever if it did come, if it did ever take me away.

Yes; but none of that ever went beyond a little fantasy with which to fill the silences between two footsteps thudding against the pavement as I walked. Never more than that. And the only result — and only sometimes — was to make me speed up toward an improvised errand, or else turn on my heels, go back home, and spend a couple of hours speeding through some task, muttering to myself that this thing, if I didn't do it now, could one day become an ulcer and damage many people and, from a distance, needle me.

In those days, it never went any further than that.

But that day, February 21, 1919, at twelve o'clock sharp, things were very different. That day, the little fantasies dreamt up so many times in the streets became reality. Certainly, there was no crane, I was not pulled from the Earth, but the effect was the same: three forces sharp as vipers bound me and swallowed me up into the new shape, separated me from my peers, and I sensed out there in the world the foul-smelling decomposition of so many things left undone, left forever in the same state I myself had been in until then: more or less at large, erratic, unoccupied; and not as they should have been left: part of a whole, an immobile, fixed element in a complete, parallel organism. And then I felt like even the closest things — the alfalfa field, those very foothills — were moving away from me. And what to say of the myrtles, the public road, and carob trees! And what of the country houses, the entire nation, the whole world! It was truly a goodbye.

But through it all I felt nothing that came close to surprise. If I had, the feeling of solemnity I'm talking about could not have arisen. And yet, at that moment, it was the only thing that existed.

Truly, the continued, almost obsessive repetition of the image of the crane had somewhat familiarized me with the idea of isolation, of death in life. But this, I repeat, had been a mere fantasy, a frivolous thing, and in and of itself it wasn't enough to eliminate surprise at passing so radically from one state to another. There was more, there had been more, and there'd been more for a long time.

Of course, when I found myself stuck there across from my two companions, I knew that in my past, in my lighthearted past of fields and cities, the possibility of suddenly becoming an elemental being had always hovered very near. And that bit about the crane was nothing but the actualization through an image — if I can explain it like that — of this vague obsession with change.

But now I recalled many acts in my life for which, in said life, I could not find a satisfying explanation. They were acts I repeated systematically, that I had to repeat, but that disintegrated once I analyzed them, sinking back into the ambiguity of something that could happen at some point or perhaps had already happened, but that in any case eluded me. So I went on with my usual daily schedule without trying to go any deeper. But the next night or the one after that I came back to the same thing, inexorably back to the same thing. I sat looking, my eyes staring, but without any clear idea forming in my brain.

And so it was, almost every night.

Almost every night, slipping from my bed, I would go down to the small living room of my house to drink a cup of coffee and then smoke, sprawled on a sofa, staring — as I've said — that is, more or less just as I was now in the funnel, the only difference being that back then I remained on the outside and was looking in at elements that were already formed, already tethered, already parallel before me; and now I only looked at, could only look at part of this new tethering, since the other part of it was me, simply me.

On the wall of the living room, facing the sofa, I had hung an artwork by Gabriela Emar that was made of two wooden planks, two pieces of metal, and three-fourths of a ring beam, all mounted on a wooden backing. Each element was colored differently with earthen paints: the first wooden plank was the most prominent shape, that is, the one closest to me, and it was, I remember, sort of triangular-shaped and a light bluish gray; then came one of the metal pieces, elongated and bent at a right angle and of an old, somewhat shiny shade of gold; behind it, like a shadow of the former, was the other piece of metal, opaque, dark, with muffled glints of ink and violet; the last shape, further back, was the other wooden plank: straight, bluish-gray like the first, but darkened and spattered here and there with a transparent paint of reddish tones; and all the way in back, biting into the others, three-fourths of a black iron circle. The backing, a burnt ocher board. On all four sides, a thin, smooth, yellowish frame.

I don't know if this gives a good idea of the piece. Well, it must still be in the house. Anyone who wants to can go and take a look.

I would spend many minutes, perhaps several quarters of an hour, staring at those shapes and letting something like a sense of equilibrium envelop me like smoke, though it did not penetrate me. I had a natural impulse or desire to transmute it into an idea, a concrete one if possible, a handheld idea I could carry with me everywhere and throw around in any direction. But at the slightest effort, the tiny roots of this idea vanished, evaporated, and, without formulating anything, I felt and knew that the elements gathered there — just as they were, as they'd already been — guaranteed a larger order, which they replicated in the stillness and silence of a small painting hung on an empty wall in my living room.

Stillness and silence ... Now I remember that I often murmured those two words to myself during those moments. They were no vain words that rose to my lips just for the pleasure of hearing them. No. Silence, stillness ... They do sound nice, to be sure, especially on nights of coffee and cigarettes. But I repeat: it wasn't that. They were spontaneous words, endpoints of an internal process that circled near my consciousness. The feeling was sharper than true silence, or true stillness. And I saw then — staring the whole time — that the stillness within that frame was like movement, since there was, first and foremost, a relationship, and a relationship can only exist if at least two things are in play, and once they are in play — the phrase says it all — they must move, since absolute stillness would make them melt together and disappear. And even if — I thought — all of that was no more than my own imagination and speculation, even if no movement existed in the picture at all, my eyes still spun in an attempt to see it, they palpated, they flickered over the wood and metal at the ends of their rays. And here there arose a difference between this particular sliding of the eyes and the way they slid over other things, other objects: with the others, with the common run of them, the sliding continued on, emptied out beyond the objects, encompassing all that surrounded them — room, house, streets, the entire world — so that objects were unable to isolate themselves, but instead continued to be details, points within the whole. Here, however, everything was enclosed, condensed within the small space limited by the frame, and moving my eyes even a hair's breadth beyond it was to definitively and inexorably leave it behind and pass to another place.

The same with the silence. With my ears attuned to the sounds and murmurs outside, the painting emanated, in contrast, silence, or rather the impossibility that its elements could produce even the most trifling vibration. In my imagination I knew that if I were ever able to penetrate that frame and listen to it from the inside, I would experience the total lack of sound. But how would I experience it? To truly understand, I had to experience it with my ears, since this was all about hearing. Then I felt that if I thought about it that way, total silence was nothing but another sort of noise, perhaps the silence of my own eardrums. But no, it wasn't that. I turned my attention from my eardrums and went on to listen again to the painting. That silence was in it and not in me. Straining my ears to their maximum, then, but concentrating energetically on quieting everything not in the painting, I tried to understand what the silence in there would sound like, and I truly heard, astounded, not just the one, but several, all the silences of each element, wood or metal, their silences that were essentially the particular way each of them had gone mute since they'd been pulled from a pile of garbage, castoffs, and junk and intertwined, placed in accord, as a mirror of the world from which they'd been separated.

Yes; all of these were things that I felt, I know it, I remember as clearly as if only a few hours had passed between the time I last contemplated the picture and today, as I write. But something else was lurking, something more insinuated itself. It was almost as if somewhere or sometime there was a certain kinship or affinity between that painting and me, or between it and my ambitions, my end goal ... or perhaps my end. One part of myself advised me to explain this thing, to attack it head-on, and in that way to learn something important. But another part of me, a slippery part, full of indolence, preferred to rock myself to sleep in the sweet sensations of stillness and silence and not expose myself to the slightest mortification in an attempt to go any deeper. The small, minuscule struggle of nearly every night. To quell it, there was always a transaction, which came in the form of a resolution, a project for the following day: a little literature will fix it all! Yes, tomorrow — I told myself — I will write that painting. For example: the story of each of its elements: the seed that led to the tree, which led to the wood; the felling of the tree, its use in this or that object; the death of the object; its passage through dust and grime; its existence in a form different from what it is today; etc., etc. And the same for the metals. Pretty stories! Along with them, soaring like an immense black bird — yes, that's how I imagined it, no more and no less: a bird that was immense, and black to boot — soaring and peering into corners of scraps and old wires, soaring: the painter's idea to pick them up, twist them, mutilate them, cut them and slit them open there, captured in color. Pretty stories!

Sometimes I felt sorry for those imprisoned elements, and I wished I could give their freedom back to them, so that they, too, could follow their destinies. It was like a frightening awareness of our own cruelty. To tie them up, to hobble them so! Just to enjoy an aesthetic sensation! And there they went on, "making a figure." The world outside . . .

But it wasn't that, no, nothing like that. As proof, the painting is there and the story was never written. And now I say to myself, I don't know why, but I say: "It wasn't written, thank God."

Those story projects were meant to delay, or more like throw off, the emerging awareness that some part of my destiny was playing a role in all that stuff about the elements. Now, scarcely had I been seated on the rock in the funnel, I saw that above those little stories, beyond any silence or stillness, I'd had a presentiment of something that was forming around me and would, one morning, give me a push and determine my life. But on those nights I could know nothing of or even suspect the existence of a cat and a flea or of myself in relation to them, so I let the presentiment pass. And back to the same: "A story of that wood and metal would be a pretty story." Just like that, all those nights at my house.

Today, summertime at noon, with cat and flea in front of me, with me in front of him and it, with all feeling of surprise quelled by so much vague prior experience, with that impression of solemnity now starting to be quelled by a quick acclimation and a defenseless resignation; now a sharp regret passed through me as I remembered my indolence, my obliviousness to so many invitations to ponder my approaching destiny, and I also felt a desolate regret for not having noticed more.

But this also passed, with astonishing speed. It had all begun as the clock struck twelve. It was still twelve o'clock and already another feeling was occupying, flooding, my entire being: terror that froze my veins.

I have said already, and I'll repeat it to the point of inanity, that from that moment on there was another whole, a living whole, organized there in the Melocotón Hills, a totality which had fallen to the side of the other one and become immediately balanced, without a single leaf in a single thicket having trembled in the process. There we were and there we remained, to the side, and because of that fact, that "to the side," there was an additional thing in the Universe. Until then, we and the forces that we were had wandered and roamed like all the rest, with few or many blows and woes, few or many gripes and indifferences, but we roamed, roamed within, amalgamated and part of the other. That was all over! Not anymore. Not from now on. I shall remind you of the date once more: February 21, 1919, at twelve o'clock sharp. Because that's still the time. It will stay that time until the full succession of my feelings has run its course. Then it will be twelve plus what comes immediately after each hour's completion.

Twelve! Terror!

Terror that, with one more totality in the Universe, the Universe could lose its equilibrium and explode.

I know what you all will say, I know you'll always try to come back to the same thing: that three cats, as much as they balance or unbalance, three cats ... etc. And I also know that no matter how much I reason, demonstrate and prove, no matter how fully I might convince all my peers, always, their feeling of cats — i.e., that in comparison with nothing less than the Cosmos itself, all cats shrink to their shabbiest expression — will prevail and triumph in any prudent, serious, and judicious man, precisely because it is a feeling.

To hell, then, with trying to make prudent men understand or vaguely suspect what it is, on one hand, to separate and remove oneself from life; on the other, to not be within but rather in front of something; and on a third hand to know — not just with the understanding but with every cell of one's skin, blood, and bones — that only equilibrium exists; and on the fourth and final hand, to hell with trying to make them see that, because nothing exists but equilibrium, nothing can be immense or minuscule; that size and conditions vanish, leaving only the equilibrium itself, without any possibility of a "plus one" or a "minus one." To hell with all that, even though basic logic should be enough to convince people of these truths. But I know, judicious men, that your feelings are stronger than anything else in you. I know that once on the verge of being convinced, you'll always throw the gear shift into reverse and say, "One cat ... two cats ... three cats ... Absurd! Impossible! Nothing will happen anywhere! There is no such equilibrium, no!"

Nevertheless, as a last resort, I can't help but make a little comparison: a scale, for example, just a scale. It is balanced and so sensitive that it doesn't makes sense to even talk about sensitivity. It is balanced, it remains, it lives, it exists in equilibrium. And suddenly a grain falls onto one of its pans, a thousandth of a grain, a millionth, less of a grain than what, on this other scale, is meant by three cats — don't forget! — intertwined and integrated. One pan will drop. Equilibrium broken!

I offer this example because as soon as I sat down, while it was still twelve o'clock, it came and pierced me like an arrow. For a moment, I even expected that the world would fall into disequilibrium. I expected the world to blow up. I waited for all the worlds to crash into each other, the little ones swallowed by the big ones, which would be, in turn — though swollen from such swallowing — swallowed by other, bigger worlds, to then be . . . Oh! In sum, by then my companions and I would be merely loose elements once again, only now we would not be wandering within an equilibrium but rather in a manifestation of imbalance.

I waited, filled with terror. But along with that terror, I noticed something like a slight universal quiver inside me. It was — or at least I felt it to be — like a circular wave starting from our center, from the Sun, and hitting the first planets, pushing them away from it just the few millimeters necessary to subsist within the new equilibrium. It hit our Earth in that moment of suspension. I felt as if my seat had shifted slightly downward, and, in the back of the cave, the cat and his flea on his forehead also shifted. And everything was reset. Then I felt the wave continue on and move the following worlds: Mars, the telescopic planets, Jupiter, and maybe Saturn. I mean: surely Saturn, too. Otherwise . . . Well, let's not go there! What I mean is that I knew nothing of Saturn; I was only guessing. Less of Uranus and Neptune. My perception picked up nothing further. Or perhaps it was already clouded by the new activity that was again emerging all around me, on all sides, from my own blood as it started to circulate again, out to infinity, starting to turn again. So that from Jupiter outwards, though I perceived nothing, I contented myself with the knowledge, with the certainty — a certainty such that no one being united with any God has ever felt — that everything, EVERYTHING, had shifted, was shifting at that moment, was balanced again, was fastened again and again went on, adjusted in a slightly different way.

At that precise second it stopped being twelve and became, as I've said, what comes immediately after each hour. Then, very far off, I heard the singing of a spotted hen bird. As its song broke very high in the sky, my ears were filled with chrysanthemums and poppies. This, and no other moment, was when a very pleasant feeling of stability flooded my entire being.

I would have omitted comparing my feelings, as they spilled out beyond Jupiter, with those I suppose must be felt by those who unite with a God, but the fidelity of my tale has gotten the better of my desire not to mention any God, as well as my certainty that none has ever meddled in my destiny. But I remember that the feeling of passing Jupiter and encompassing the infinite cosmos was, I thought and firmly believed, the same as what is felt by all who claim to have merged with divinity. Perhaps because I was tired or because it was never repeated, however, I started to doubt myself until I forgot about the feeling entirely. Now I remember it again and dutifully record it.

Twelve o'clock has struck. Everything for everyone resumes its usual pace and I, in my utter stability, notice that the hours pass lightly for me. Me, him, it ... It, him, me ... Him, it, me ... This occupies me, absorbs me. Hours pass. Days pass. I feel that my entire previous life has definitively disappeared.

But don't get the idea that there were no disruptions. Once several months had passed, I often fell prey to nostalgia. My home, my people, my life as an untethered man! To push them away from me and recover the stability of my new state was a painful labor, especially when I was struck by the memory of that morning when, unworried, with no errand at all, I'd had Tinterillo saddled up and we'd headed out toward those hills. My last morning! That's why I wrote about it in such detail. Extreme temperatures, useful smells, human smells, the pimpano, the quilehue, the tench fava, the devil's dog and swamp kissing bugs ... And finally the huge Andean buzzard and the trilling waterfalls of those spotted hen birds one never sees. But again stability ruled me, again I was wrapped up in our equilibrium, and more than that, more than anything, by our purpose, our dreadful responsibility, as it was just us three, cat, flea, and me, hidden away there on the mountainside, who were the counterweight, or more like the counterpart – the mirror! – of the whole.

Years passed, and our lives were reduced to the most minimal movements. The flea occasionally bit the cat, spent the rest of the time sleeping, and very rarely moved a few millimeters. The cat, sitting down, looked at me, stretched out, arched its back, slept little and never meowed. I, seated as well, would sit a little straighter, stretch out my legs, pull them back in; I don't think I've slept this whole time. And with each of our movements, slight as they may be, the triangle obeyed with a certain rigidity, a certain hard flexibility. I seemed to hear, then, a sort of creaking, like the friction of wet ropes.

And at times I felt desperation, the horrible desperation of finding myself stuck there. I had sudden urges that came very close to madness, the urge to jump up and start running, to plunge down the hill and dive into the vast alfalfa field as though it were a lake, an ocean. To insert myself back into the living world with those violet flowers – life, once again – to chew them, suck and tear at them. To jump up and take off – come what may! – to jump and run. But whenever those desires spurred me on, the cat turned his green eyes my way and drained them of their shine, soothing me with a look that was muted, soft, and placid, and he shredded all my plans of escape.

Then I raged at that damned animal. I slowly reached for my gun. It would be so simple to take aim. The muzzle would be right on the line between him and me; the bullet would travel its full length and blow the lid off his brains, blasting the damned flea along the way. Of course, I've never fired. The three of us are still just as we were in that summer of '19. I have never fired and nor, I think, will I ever, since two conjectures have stayed my hand and will stay it in the future. Here they are:

1) As the bullet entered the animal's skull, our entire equilibrium would be broken. Of this there can be no doubt. Nor can

there be any doubt that, once it is broken, all that surrounded us would be thrown out of balance, causing a wider imbalance, and that imbalance would cause another until it led to a complete breakdown. Our organism, here in the funnel, is so sensitive and precise that it could not be toppled with impunity – it would mean exposing ourselves to greater consequences, exposing ourselves to chaos.

I then objected, to rile myself up, that if in the first instance, when our new equilibrium was created, the cosmos had adjusted to it, now, for the same reason, the old equilibrium would return with no further consequence than a slight universal shift in the opposite direction. And, as such, blessed peace for all and for the corpses of my silent companions!

No, that's not how it would go! First I doubted; then came the opposite certainty. The revolver returned to its holster. I reasoned as follows:

The first time, the funnel had formed without any personal will. Without it! Herein lies the difference, here all the axes of the matter converged: with no personal will, without the involvement of any man's will. And since I could not and still cannot conceive of anything being made manifest without a guiding will, then it follows that the guiding will on that morning was beyond any design of mine. Therefore, it was fate, quite simply. And the three of us were merely fate's agents. As such, the thing was preordained, it fit in with the order of things. Everything, for eons, had been shaping and preparing itself for that moment when three beings would join in a new channel of life, when three beings would break off, adding another weight to the balance.

This time, though, it would have been the will of a man. And this particular man could not realize his will with full control of his faculties, because any attempt on his part was shredded as soon as he received the slow gaze of a cat with muted green eyes. He would have to be seized by a fit of utter disorder, of madness, in order to make it happen. Such a man, up against destiny! The very insignificance of the agent proved that the task could not be undertaken. In any case, not by this man.

And my reasoning went on:

The fit comes, madness, the bullet fires ... Last time, the destiny gestated had been delivered with the slight quivering of a suspended instant. This time, no gestation, nothing was preordained: it would be a surprise. And that would cause the funnel to creak, and the creak would grow, increasing from place to place, from world to world, until: downfall, chaos!

No to the revolver. We go on. Me, him, it ... It, me, him ... Him, it, me ...

It's for the best.

2) Nothing happens, absolutely nothing. The triangle is broken by a bullet or by anything else. Let's suppose the most violent method: dynamite, and everything goes flying; or the calmest: I get up from the rock, stretch, brush off my clothes, and walk away, putting one foot after the other. And nothing happens, not here or anywhere else. For some reason I don't understand — after all, I can't know everything — the old equilibrium is suddenly reestablished, and no one notices the slight quiver, not even me, as I'm already captivated by the sight of the foothills and the distant fields. I return, retracing my steps back to the country houses, and I am once again an elongated force, personally unconcerned with equilibriums, and concerned only with my own personal life.

This would not be possible.

A few moments of meditation are enough for me to be sure of the absolute impossibility.

I would again be an unoccupied force. Everything might go back to being more or less as before — but not exactly as before. During the period of having once been and being once more, something must have happened. Things go back to what they were, but with the imprint of what has happened. In my case:

that unoccupied force, which would go back to roaming, would have learned what it is to be, would have acquired an awareness of a different state, of the possibility of its occupation, of its subsistence. Its nature would be fundamentally different, much as it might appear the same.

Now, there can be no doubt that the difference would be that of a superior state fallen to an inferior one. We must not think of me as a person, one who either walks freely along roads and highways or is stuck here at the funnel's mouth. That could lead us into error, because striding around will seem to be superior to remaining nearly motionless on a rock, and then the process will be seen as the opposite of what it is. In this, I am, I repeat, no more than a mere agent. It's the forces that express themselves through us that I want to talk about; in particular, my own force. That's what this is about.

Now that force would be loose once again, but not exactly as before. Now it would have something extra, something like what in humans is called memory or experience — the memory or experience of being superior. What is referred to as nostalgia or longing would hover enmeshed within it. I don't know how. But it would be there. As a simple material ductility or as a subtle moral tendency ... I don't know. But there it would be.

Here in my hideaway, I can't find any other word: tendency. A tendency to be embodied once more, to not continue circulating, to threaten the great equilibrium. And if there is something conscious about it, then it wouldn't be merely a tendency, but there would also be fear. Fear that the force's accelerating idleness, upon colliding with the other two, who would be idly accelerating as well, would cause the breakdown, laboriously avoided until that morning and now conjured, imprisoned, in me, in him, and in it.

It would irk, it would lurk, it would seep until finding. And — tendency or longing — it would lean toward me, who had removed this element from an indestructible whole and returned it to its idleness of endless trotting about.

It would be, then, an obsession that filled my every moment. It would seem to me that every evil occurrence anywhere would be, somehow, my fault. At every catastrophe, even every inclemency, I would never stop saying to myself — much as I hurried my steps down streets and highways — that if I had only stayed there in the Melocotón Hills maintaining the little parallel world, inclemencies and even catastrophes could have been avoided. I could not go on living without shouldering the weight of even the imperceptible creakings of nature as it unfolded in its suffering.

Then, what would be my salvation, my idée fixe? What would I impose upon myself in order to be free, to pardon so much guilt?

Return! Go back to the funnel!

At this point in my thoughts I sensed a possible solution:

Leave this place; if, once I was out in the world, the world distracted and pardoned me, I could remain there and record the funnel episode as one more memory; if the force pursued me and intensified my obsession, I'd return. At least that way I would know that there was not nor could there ever be any other choice for me. I would know the power of my condition, and it would perhaps calm my rage toward the cat, allowing me to return sans revolver.

But let's look at this calmly.

First point:

Who would dare assure me that once I was far away, the cat, with his flea on his forehead, would stay here? Isn't it logical that he would also leave and I would lose him forever? Any serious reasoning must lead to this conclusion: if I, up to then, had not moved because the two of them were in front of me, they had also not moved because I was in front of them. From which we can deduce that if I leave, they will leave too. So: I would return to an empty funnel and nothing could be formed again.

My life, then, would turn into a desperate search for my cat ... or another cat. My life would become a cat chase.

Second point:

I get a cat. What's more: fate is so kind as to offer me a cat with a flea right on his forehead. Here I am, then, on my way to the Melocotón Hills. My horse, another Tintorillo, gallops. My old one must be dead. My cat comes along in a sack. We gallop. Our needs send us their scents; humans, as well; plants in the myrtles, creatures in the myrtles; the alfalfa field, and another greeting to that incomparable Chinese friend, Fa; spotted hen birds and buzzards. The funnel!

Third point:

I crawl into the funnel with my cat in my hands to place him in the niche at the back. I place him there. He stays. I crawl back like a reptile. I stand, turn around, and walk to the rock.

As I take the first step, the cat will jump out of the niche and follow on my heels. Then ... I turn around, pick him up, to the niche once again.

I back up, turn around, and ... the cat on my heels! And once again, and again, again and again. In vain will I pet him there in the niche, convincing him to remain completely still. As soon as he sees my heels, to the ground and after them!

Now my heels are starting to acquire a special sensitivity. Now I exist solely in this part of my body. They are now two wounds. And the cat doesn't stop.

I back up without turning around. He hesitates a moment, but ultimately jumps down. And he comes, he comes, he seeks out my heels, winding around my feet. To avoid him, I move toward the niche. Him, behind me. But the funnel's narrowness forces me to stop. If I crawl on the ground, the cat will get at my heels. Back outside then. Out! Out! The cat will throw me out — out into the world of obsessions once again! Or maybe all the years I have left to live will consist of this coming and going to the niche, to the cave's mouth, to the niche, to the mouth. And by now heels and cat would be one — painful, bloody, horrible!

The years pass, they pass. The three of us stay motionless here, cat, flea, and man.

It's best, indisputably, not to unleash what has been bound. It's best for this new mirror of life to continue its course from me to him, from him to it, from it to me. To hell with other men and the other Universe!

We'll be right here.

Anyway, what's all the fuss about? As I've said, our triangle has a certain flexibility. We move a little, we stretch. The flea sleeps sometimes; the cat arches his back; I cross my legs, fold and separate my hands at will. There is freedom. For example, right now the cat is sleeping. I'm taking that chance to commit our lives to writing, today, on May 30, 1934.

May ...

Another autumn, another winter. The spotted hen birds, more than singing, let out freezing squawks. The Andean buzzards fly toward the sea covered in white feathers.

We're still here.

The Trained Dog

DESIDERIUS LONGOTOMA, WOLDEMAR LONQUIMAY, and I are friends. Nothing strange about that, since we played together as children.

Was what we did really playing? For Desiderius Longotoma and me, yes it was. For Woldemar Lonquimay ... doubtful. Woldemar Lonquimay was, even as a child, extremely serious and reflective, and he was, moreover ...

Well, I have already written an outline of the psychological substrata of his being, and one of these days I will publish it. To repeat it all here would only annoy me.

In our youth, the three of us set out on our first escapades.

Oat sowing? I might add the same caveat here as I did for our childhood games, with Desiderius Longotoma and I on one hand, Woldemar Lonquimay on the other.

When we were twenty, more or less, Desiderius Longotoma bought a newborn puppy and trained it. He named it Piticuti. Piticuti was small, with a long, dark brown body.

Desiderius Longotoma said to us one day, "Every passerby is an absurdity. Any human being, when he sits still or pursues his activities or satisfies his vital needs, is potentially reasonable. But the moment he becomes a passerby, he is absurd. Friends, we must avenge this absurdity!"

So we did as follows:

Every night, in a dark room on the ground floor of my house — whose window onto the street is protected by iron bars — the three of us and the dog would crouch down.

Silence. A long wait. Mine was a quiet street.

Suddenly, a passerby. He passed by the window. Desiderius Longotoma murmured, "Hup!"

Piticuti lunged, barking at the bars. The passerby just about fainted. This went on every night for over a month.

Another day he told us, "All of this revenge is taken on the hearts of passersby. It is revenge by means of a feeling, which is what fright is. Well, that's not enough! We must take vengeance with pain. Friends, at their legs!"

And we went out at night, the three of us and the dog, to traverse the secluded streets.

We decided that the sixteenth passerby to cross our paths would be our victim; then the thirty-second; then the forty-eighth. Always by sixteens.

When a victim passed, Desiderius Longotoma would mutter, "Hup!"

And Piticuti would bite an ankle. Then the four of us would flee.

Upon going out each night, I would wonder with indescribable anxiety, "Who will be the sixteenth? What will he look like? What were his occupations and preoccupations during the day? Which of those has driven him out into the streets at night? If he is a man, has he a wife? If he has one, does he love her? And if he is a woman? (For we did not absolve women; a woman who takes to the sidewalk is just as much a passerby as a man). Returning home, will she be greeted by a child who is indifferent to her injury? Or by a little old lady who fusses over it to the point of hysteria? Or two jocular friends who will laugh at the ridiculousness of it all? Or will no one at all be there to greet her?"

The same questions for the thirty-second, the forty-eighth, etc.

Sometimes there were substitutions that heightened my anxiety to the point of anguish:

The sixteenth is coming. Suddenly, he turns and walks back the way he came. This was not his fate.

The sixteenth is coming. Suddenly, from around a corner, another passerby gets ahead of the former, and now he is the sixteenth. He has snatched the fatal number for himself.

It was his fate, not the other's.

Etc.

Anguish suffocates. Anguish, like suffocation — if you look closely — is permeated with voluptuousness. Hence the stories of people who have been on the verge of drowning. Hence the longing — seemingly paradoxical — for certain past periods of our lives when we lived in the clutches of anguish.

All of this is voluptuousness.

But let us summarize, at least in what pertains to me.

The sum total of these outings was for me a suffocating sense of destiny.

Because I felt the reality of destiny, its living existence, like a monster that, though invisible, loomed — heavy, mute, and sullen — over the city.

It was a monster made of threads.

Those threads went weaving themselves together through all the streets.

Every passerby trailed a thread along behind him, at times like a slug's silvery slime, at others like the fine strand a spider expels.

These threads were visible to the passersby as experiences, as memories. Me, I could almost see them with my eyes. For me, they were visible on the border between inner and outer sight.

Sometimes I saw them — externalized, pure — all along the black streets, trembling.

At the end of each, a person walked.

All the passersby spun another thread ahead of them. It was only visible to them as volition, as desire. Along this thread, unlike the other, unforeseen events lay in ambush.

We were "unforeseen events" for all the beings who walked the city!

But we had no direct contact with them. We needed another creature, of another species: Piticuti.

These threads were scarcely visible to me. I saw them only looking head-on. On the other hand, my sense of touch perceived them better than the ones behind, for I clearly felt them pierce my body like very long, thin needles.

One night I noticed with alarm that they all pierced me, or tended to, right through my sex.

I tried to communicate this observation to my friends. Desiderius Longotoma laughed and laughed his usual laugh; Woldemar Lonquimay, grave as marble, was unmoved.

I communicated nothing to them.

And Piticuti bit again.

Eventually, all that abuse of our fellow citizens started to weigh on our consciences.

To absolve ourselves, we decided to pool our money. We divided the sum total into four equal parts, to be lovingly offered to the sixteenth, thirty-second, forty-eighth, and sixty-fourth pedestrian.

And we headed to the city's poorest neighborhood.

Piticuti stayed locked up at home.

Astonished, I realized that I felt no threads behind, no threads ahead, and no sex.

I knew that giving away money had to produce the same effect as violence. I knew it ... that's all.

I don't know what my friends' experience was. All I know is that Woldemar Lonquimay said, "This good deed is worthless."

And Desiderius Longotoma: "Let's go for a drink. Enough of this nonsense!"

And the next night we went right back to our marauding adventures with Piticuti.

Another time, Desiderius Longotoma told us with a mysterious air, "I have a new project to undertake with our faithful companion. Tomorrow I shall solemnly tell you."

But the next morning, Piticuti woke up dead.

We buried him in the yard of his owner's house. We piled dirt over his body. Over the dirt, we placed a cement headstone.

Desiderius Longotoma fell into a deep sadness. He refused to tell us what his project was, and would only repeat, "Now ... what's the point?"

And I never again felt the profound, heartrending sensuousness of those nocturnal, trembling threads.

Poor Piticuti!

Twenty-three years later.

One week ago today.

I felt it again!

I was walking toward the hill in the center of this city. It was eight o'clock at night. Many passersby were out, many cars, busses, and trams. Lights and neon signs shone. It was dizzying.

On the left side of the hill there is a tangled maze of narrow streets that has only grown more tangled as new alleyways and plazas are opened and huge residential complexes are built.

But I know this neighborhood well.

My intention was to reach one of those buildings, where a woman who unsettles and attracts me has an apartment.

Suddenly, just meters from the hill, I became confused.

I hesitated for a hundredth of a second. All those streets seemed to run together, entangled in a jumble so sudden and unexpected that I was pierced by a sharp feeling of mystery — dark, frightful, effervescent — emanating from the whole neighborhood.

And in that bubbling mystery, She was there.

She was living it with her entire body. With her sex.

And I, despite jumbles and mazes, would keep going, and I'd arrive like a sleepwalker, borne aloft by an anguished voluptuousness.

Then the whole neighborhood, writhing with Her, ricocheted off my sex.

I had felt it again!

For the space of a hundredth of a second, sure. No matter.

I felt again!

And I learned that there is a clear relationship between a city's configuration and our most hidden desires. Just as I had learned in the past (thanks to Piticuti's fangs) that from a certain point of view, there is also a clear relationship between said desires and the beings who walk the streets.

Then I had the idea to return to our old companion's grave, and to leave something there, an offering in his memory.

But what?

I don't know.

Every idea I've come up with has quickly presented several flaws.

Now I think the best thing would be to place a snail on one end of the headstone. And to stand there, motionless, until it crosses the whole thing end to end; to stay there until it disappears from sight, far away — hopefully in the sea.

The Unicorn

DESIDERIUS LONGOTOMA IS THE MOST ABSENT-MINDED man in this city. He found himself obliged to send the following notice to all the newspapers:

"Yesterday, between four and five o'clock in the afternoon, in the area bounded on the N. by calle de los Perales, to the S. by Taja-mar, to the E. by calle del Rey and to the W. by calle del Macetero Blanco, I lost my best ideas and my purest intentions, that is, my personality as a man. I will give a magnificent reward to whoever finds it and brings it to my home, calle de la Nevada, 101."

That very day, I scoured the area he'd indicated. After a long search, I found a cow's molar in a trash can. I didn't hesitate even for an instant. I picked it up and headed for 101 Nevada.

Eleven people were waiting in line in front of Desiderius Lon-gotoma's house. Each of them held something in their hands, cherishing the certainty that it was the human personality lost the day before.

The first had: a small jar of sand;
the second: a live lizard;
the third: an old ivory-handled umbrella;
the fourth: a couple of raw prairie oysters;
the fifth: a flower;
the sixth: a false beard;
the seventh: a microscope;

the eighth: a moorhen's feather;
the ninth: a bottle of perfume;
the tenth: a butterfly;
the eleventh: their own son.

Desiderius Longotoma's butler ushered us in one by one.

Desiderius Longotoma was standing at the back of his living room. Same as always: cheerful, stocky, with his little black mustache, affable and mild.

He accepted everything that was brought to him, and generously handed out the rewards he had promised.

To the first he gave: a penknife;
to the second: two cigars;
to the third: a rattle;
to the fourth: a rubber sponge;
to the fifth: a stuffed lynx;
to the sixth: a strip of blue velvet;
to the seventh: a couple of baked eggs;
to the eighth: a small clock;
to the ninth: a rabbit trap;
to the tenth: a key chain;
to the eleventh: a pound of sugar;
to me: a gray tie.

Three days later I visited Desiderius Longotoma. I wanted to sound him out on a few points that are not worth mentioning here.

Desiderius Longotoma was in bed. In a wire net hung above the headboard and extending to the middle of the bed, he had placed the twelve objects representing our twelve beliefs about his lost personality.

Beneath all this, Desiderius Longotoma was meditating.

(A passing observation: the cow molar hung just above his sternum.)

This sheltered meditation reminded me of the advice I had received from this same character on October 1 last year under a coral tree.

After a long silence, Desiderius Longotoma said to me, "I wish to enter into wedlock. I can only meditate in the shadow of something. I would like to marry so as to meditate in the shade of two horns. I've decided on Matilde Atacama, the widow of the late Rudecindo Malleco. This woman, her matchless beauty aside, has taken to cerebral lovemaking. Since I don't know a thing about that, it won't be long before Matilde gives me a cuckold's horns. My only worry is her choice of a lover. For there are men who, upon possessing another's wife, cause the husband's forehead to sprout the horns of a bull; others, those of a billy goat; others, a buck; others, a buffalo; others, a moose; still others, a bighorn sheep ... In sum, every sort that zoology has to offer. And I wish to meditate under the large antlers of a buck. That's all."

I hinted, "Do you think I ... ?"

He replied, "Absolutely not. You would make me sprout the single horn of a unicorn."

The unicorn lives in faraway jungles in the confines of Ethiopia.

The unicorn feeds solely on the fragrant petals of sleeping water lilies.

That fact notwithstanding, its excrement smells extremely foul.

The unicorn, in its leisure time, uses its single horn to dig vast caves in the soft earth of swamps. From the ceilings of these caves hang amber stalactites, and hairy spiders on silvery threads.

The unicorn cannot be tamed. When it sees a man, it evaporates entirely, except for its horn, which falls to the ground standing upright. Then the horn sprouts serrated leaves and fleshy fruits, and is thenceforth known as "The Tree of Repose."

This fruit, when mixed with milk, becomes the most violent of poisons for young women in flower. Marcel Proust was unaware of this fact. Had he known, he could have saved himself a few tomes.

Women who die in this way do not decompose. They are turned

into marble for all eternity. The man who gazes on their marble form forever loses all interest in any woman who speaks, breathes, and moves through space.

I don't see why all this about the unicorn would be contrary to Desiderius Longotoma's intentions.

Desiderius Longotoma insists, "Buck antlers! That's it!"

There was a knock at the door. An old woman entered. In her hands she held a piece of clay in which was stuck, by the heel, a well-worn ladies' shoe; inside the shoe, a verse by Espronceda.

Deciderio Longotoma thanked her cheerfully, bestowed on her as recompense a scroll and an oyster, and, when the lady was gone, he skewered the whole thing on the tip of the ivory-handled umbrella. Then he repeated, "Buck antlers! That's it!"

Desiderius Longotoma has entered into wedlock with Matilde Atacama.

Matilde Atacama has taken a lover who has made the horns of a buck sprout from Desiderius Longotoma's head. Thus, the man can now meditate in peace.

After his meditations, he did the following:

He bought a grinder machine, model XY 6, eight cylinders, hydraulic pressure, and threw into it the thirteen treasures that we gave him when he lost his personality. And he ground them up.

He crushed and ground them into a fine, homogenous powder. Then he placed the powder in a hermetically sealed retort that he exposed, for five minutes, to the light of the Moon.

While he was doing that, Matilde Atacama was in her lover's arms, and I was finishing up preparations for a trip to the faraway confines of Ethiopia.

* *

I set sail from Valparaíso on the S.S. *Orangutan*, and thirty-seven days later I alighted in Alexandria.

I continued on to Cairo. A visit to the pyramids.

At night, a visit to the observatory. I spent a long time gazing at magnificently shimmering Sirius, which I recognized because I'd seen it from the San Cristóbal observatory four years earlier. Then I gazed at the Moon. I also recognized its mountains — one in particular, like a monolith, alone, defenseless, in the middle of an immense desert that looked like ice or milk.

Along with this recognition, I was suddenly seized by doubt regarding the truth that Cairo and Santiago are two spatially distinct places. The idea of spacial simultaneity won out: first Sirius and the lunar mountains hinted at it, then it expanded and filled me as that white monolith passed into my eyesight.

The next day, a second visit to the pyramids. With the tip of my cane I rapped repeatedly on a stone at the base of the Cheops pyramid. With each rap, the idea beamed down by the Moon disintegrated, and Cairo and my hometown split apart and were once more separated by oceans and continents.

I continued onward down the Nile by sailboat, then on camelback over all kinds of plateaus, and, three months after leaving Santiago, I reached the confines of Ethiopia.

Two days of rhythmic exercises to get used to the climate, and, ready! Here's how:

I crouched down at the foot of a birch tree, with a jug of water on one side, on the other some regional bread rolls; above my head an automatic alarm clock that rang as soon as I got tired, and, at my feet, a portrait of a naked woman I had previously pierced with a wolf's fang and hung on a sixteenth-century chasuble. And I waited, I waited ... 24 hours, 48 hours, 96 hours, 192 hours, and ...

Graceful, agile, svelte, sibilant, luminous, from amid the jungle's green stepped a magnificent specimen of a unicorn.

Now I had only to shout and, once I had its attention, it would see me and evaporate. I shouted, "Present arrrrr . . . !!"

The unicorn turned, looked at me, and evaporated. And as its horn fell to the ground, the portrait of the naked woman crumpled, and a macaw sang.

The horn dug in and buried its base. Minutes later it sprouted serrated leaves; hours later it produced a beautiful fleshy red fruit. With a pair of long scissors I cut it off, wrapped it in the chasuble, and, my mission complete, I strode off toward the Red Sea.

There, a submarine was waiting for me. We traveled back through the ocean's depths, passing beneath the continents, which allowed me to make two observations. One: no continent, not one of the planetary landmasses, is attached; they all float. Two: the Earth does not rotate; the Earth itself is completely motionless on its axis; only this layer of water enwrapping it, on which the continents float, turns; however, its nucleus (that is, nearly all of the planet) — I repeat — does not turn.

When I offered this latter observation to the First Engineer, he looked at me for a while, smiled, then tapped me on the shoulder and went off to his cabin. A minute later he came back with a tennis ball that he spun around with his fingers. He asked me, "Does it or does it not rotate?"

I replied, "Certainly."

"Well then," he went on, "it's the same with the Earth: given that the ball's rubber and its felt casing rotate, what difference does it make what happens to the emptiness inside? The ball rotates and that's that. To claim otherwise, my friend, is to split hairs."

"Allow me, esteemed First Engineer. If that ball had, let's say, another, wooden ball inside it, and when you moved your fingers, you made the outer ball turn and slide over the inner one, does the whole thing turn? I would say: no. And such, I believe, is the case with the Earth."

"You are wrong, my friend. The Earth is like this ball and not the one you're picturing. There is nothing inside it, it is empty."

"Is that possible?"

"Very possible. Just put a little thought into it: consider that if there were something inside, like that fire one hears so much about, or those circles of demons and vermin your friend Desiderius Longotoma likes so much, or whatever else it may be, do you think that we men would be the sad and ruined beings that we are? Do you think we would wander like this, brooding, between pain, misery, and love? Certainly not, my friend. You can be sure that a light would shine in our proud foreheads. The inside of the Earth is emptiness."

I turned to the First Navigator. He told me, "You are in the right. The inside of the Earth is immobile on its axis, it does not turn. What turns is this layer of water with solids floating on its surface."

"And yet," I dared to suggest, "there are those who say that beyond these waters there is absolutely nothing."

"Wrong," he replied. "The whole interior is made up of a dark, compact, inviolable metal; a hard, mute metal. Were it not so, if there was in fact an immense emptiness that could be traversed and explored by birds and spirits, do you think that we men would be as gloomy and anguished as we are? No, sir. A divine smile would adorn our faces forever, and the scowl of sorrow would be utterly unknown to us. Inside the Earth there is only metal, black and heavy as destiny."

"Whatever is there," I said, "I would like to know something else, esteemed First Navigator: Why does a submarine such as this one have a tennis ball aboard?"

"That, my good sir," he replied, "you will never know."

And with that, he walked away.

Our voyage continued. Twenty-eight days after leaving the coasts of the Red Sea, we crossed beneath the Andes. From below, we saw the enormous crater of Quizapu as a bleak, pockmarked tube. It was nighttime, and we caught a glimpse, through the volcano's open mouth, of a passing comet that seemed to crown it.

As we moved into the waters of the Pacific, we surfaced for the first time. Half a mile away, a skiff from the Caleuche ghost ship was passing by with a crew of three dead warlocks. On the submarine's deck, an argument took place. The First Engineer stated, "Those three cadavers are of the masculine sex, since, as you all must know, as long as the Caleuche has existed — that is, ever since God separated the waters from the land — it has been formally established that no dead witch would ever man any of its skiffs."

The First Navigator made a face, and, asking the Captain for the spyglass, he said solemnly, "Just a moment."

He looked for a long time. Then he said, "Esteemed First Engineer, you are mistaken. The third cadaver, the one in the stern, is of the female persuasion. My friend," he turned to me, "see for yourself that I am right."

And he handed me the spyglass.

In truth, that cadaver was indeed smaller than the other two. From its decayed skull hung long locks that were more reminiscent of the hair of a being that had been feminine in life, and under its rags I could see a soft, jellylike matter in its chest, and not the hard ribs of the other two.

These observations did not put an end to the discussion. The First Engineer exclaimed, "My esteemed First Navigator, don't contradict me. My scientific knowledge regarding the Caleuche is complete. I'll prove it: right now, it is 2:38 a.m. So, since a force three northeastern wind is blowing, and since there are only two clouds in the sky and not a fish in sight, the Caleuche must therefore appear two hours and seventeen minutes after the sighting of one of its embarkations, crewed by three cadavers."

We waited.

In effect, at 4:55 a.m., we saw to port the tips of the Caleuche's oars, and, under the water, the gleam of its submarine lights.

The First Engineer's science was profound, no doubt about it. Still, the First Navigator would not let his arm be twisted, and he merely smiled devilishly. Then he called me aside and whispered into my ear, "The First Engineer knows a lot, an enormous amount, about the relationship of time and distance between the Caleuche and its embarkations. But when it comes to the sex of the cadavers crewing the latter, believe me, he is perfectly ignorant."

And with no further ado, we went into the submarine and submerged once again.

Two days later we arrived in Valparaíso.

I traveled by car to Santiago that very night.

At two in the morning, I am standing in front of my house with the chasuble and the fleshy fruit under my arm as the car speeds off.

And another story begins.

Not a minute had passed when I was overcome by a desire to open my door with a different key, to enter on tiptoe in the utmost silence, with a long pause after each step, trembling at the noise of the rats, and to steal, to steal as much as I could from my own house.

That's what I did.

From a closet, I took a broad black cloth in which to carry the stolen objects. In my office I have Sarah Bernhardt's skull; I stole it from myself. In the hall I have a painting by Luis Vargas Rosas; I stole it. In the dining room I have two antique salt shakers made of gold; I stole them. And scattered around all the corners of the house I have the complete works of Don Diego Barros Arana; I stole them from myself, too.

I reached my bedroom.

At that hour, on that day — if Desiderius Longotoma had never mentioned the unicorn to me — I would have been in bed asleep. On that day and at that hour, if a thief had come into my bedroom after ransacking half the house, I would have awakened, and, sitting bolt upright in my sheets, shouted: "Who goes there?" And that's exactly how I woke up and shouted.

And if I were ever to ransack the bedroom of an honest citizen and hear his alarmed voice ring out in the night, I would crouch down behind a wardrobe and wait anxiously, reaching my hand out for a weapon — in this case, the long scissors that, in the confines of Ethiopia, I had used to cut the fruit from the tree of quietude. And thus I hid and my hand armed itself. Silence.

In the silence, I shouted again: "Who goes there?"

I gripped the scissors. My panting echoed off the panels of the wardrobe that hid me from view.

From my bed, I heard his panting. Not a moment to lose! I leapt out of bed, grabbed my gun from the drawer of my bedside table, and — light!

Catching myself by surprise in the light, I didn't hesitate. I pounced like a leopard, the point of the scissors raised high.

Finding myself thus attacked, I aimed and fired.

Seeing the muzzle, I made a quick dodge. The bullet grazed my right temple and hit the mirror in front of me. Then I took the scissors and struck with all the strength of my arm, plunging them into my belly.

I was wounded, stabbed, and the gun slipped from my hand as I fell stretched out on the floor.

I took the chance to deliver a second scissor stab, and this time I went for the heart.

With my heart pierced, I expired.

It was 2:37 in the morning.

Facing my bleeding, lifeless body, I retreated with cautious steps. I thought then of Scarpia's stiff body as Tosca backed away.

I crossed the threshold of the house again, walking backwards. Again I smelled the damp asphalt. A name resonated in the silence of my skull: Camila!

I took shelter that night in a hotel, any hotel. I repeated: Camila! I slept.

The next day, the papers announced my death in large print, headlining the articles with these words:

The day after that, the papers gave the details of my solemn funeral rites.

Once I was buried on my back beneath the grass, cockroaches and ants, my empty skull again echoed with the revered name of Camila, Camila. Camila!

Then I thought how Marcel Proust didn't know about the fruit of the tree of quietude, mixed with a little milk.
    Camila!
    I dialed her phone number: 52061.
    Camila!

I had always reproached Camila — as she laughed and jibed at me — for her absolute ignorance. Until a few days ago, Camila thought that almond shells were made by specialized carpenters to protect the nut inside; that Hitler and Stalin were two personages with close ties to our National Congress; that rats were spontaneously born from trash piled up in basements; that Mussolini was an Argentine citizen; that the Battle of Yungay had been fought in 1914 on the Franco-Belgian border. Camila lived outside of all reality, outside of any facts. Camila was oblivious, as such, to my shocking murder and gloomy burial. And so, when she saw me arrive at her house, she ran happily toward me with arms outstretched, carefree as a newborn animal.
    Then, laughing exuberantly, she pointed to the chasuble under my arm and cried, "What, so you're a priest now?"
    Then, before her astonished eyes, I unwrapped the magnificent red fruit and showed it to her.
    "Is it edible?" she asked.
    When I nodded, she took it in her hands, and in a long, soft, wet caress, licked it top to bottom with her throbbing little tongue.

Then she made as if to sink her teeth into it. I stopped her.

"Not like that. It could be bad for you. We have to mix it with milk."

When you're lying flat under the ants and cockroaches in a cemetery, all feeling of responsibility disappears.

That feeling is activated and takes root when other men point at you in the street as you go by.

But if you're laid out flat, there's not a finger that can perforate a funerary headstone.

We both ate of the fleshy red fruit. Except that she was a young woman in flower.

I laid Camila's marble corpse atop the very table upon which we'd dined, and, very slowly — finally — I undressed it. I now did to her precisely what she had done to the fruit moments before, from her hair to her feet. Then I wrapped her in the big black cloth I had taken from the wardrobe (now an empty rag, for the stolen objects had tumbled onto the sidewalks as I went from my house to the hotel murmuring the revered name of Camila).

Back on the sidewalk, hefting her marble weight. In her house, in the different spaces she occupied in life, there are still bits of the sixteenth-century chasuble, and, on her bed, the long scissors.

Desiderius Longotoma does gymnastics every morning. Then he bathes in water heated to thirty-nine degrees Celsius. Then, for no less than half an hour, he rubs his chest and extremities with the fine, homogenous powder he gets from his XY 6 grinder (eight cylinders, hydraulic pressure).

"This does wonders for the health," he told me when he saw me. "Shame you'll never get to enjoy this massage, because you have an admirable memory. Thanks to the weakness of mine, you see, I can endure the rigors of winter, the summer heat, big meals, strong drink, tobacco, and love, as if they were nothing at all."

His rubdown over, he got dressed and took great pains with his toilette. He put a flower in his buttonhole. He walked to his salon. Lit a cigar. Crossed his legs. Rubbed his hands together. Then he asked me, "What brings you here?"

The black cloth fell.

"Camila!"

White, cold, hard nakedness, wrought so indecorously as to bring the highest degree of pleasure.

Past midnight, like two mysterious rogues, Desiderius Longotoma and I left 101 Nevada carrying Camila's remains; he took the feet and I the head. Back to the sidewalks for a third time.

Halfway there, at my request, we switched places: he took the head and I the feet. For I have always found Camila's feet to be a subject for much deeper meditations than her hair.

An hour later we entered the cemetery.

Ten minutes after that we found my grave, and could imagine the sordid decomposition of my viscera under the stone.

Desiderius Longotoma prayed for a long time in a low, hurried voice.

Then we pulled up the cross from my grave and headed to that of Julián Ocoa, who had always been a good man and a distinguished violinist. Because he had never believed in God or his only son Jesus Christ, we placed it there.

Then we picked up Camila, momentarily left on the grass. We raised her upright and buried her little feet in the place where, moments before, the bottom of the cross had stood.

This time, both of us prayed, plus a cricket.

The next day, the city's artists discussed this new sculpture.

There were those who found it too boldly naturalistic; others, overly stylized. There were those who traced it to Athens; others to Byzantium; others to Florence; others to Paris. There were those who considered it offensive to make the pubescent body of a virgin shine onto the departed; there were those who averred that the nudity of a young girl in bloom could redeem all the sins of those who slept underground. There was one who threw a thistle at her feet; another, an orchid; another, a gob of spit; another, a handful of coral and mother-of-pearl.

I watched it all from behind a cypress tree; Desiderius Longotoma, crouched down in an empty grave.

Three days later, artists no longer opined about Camila's marble. Then came the winter, and the freezing rain ran down her pure form that gazed up at the clouds.

Two hours before the Sun rises from behind the Andes, I walk, every day, with plodding steps, to the cemetery.

I stand in front of my grave and Camila. Motionless, I meditate.

I want my meditation to be profound. I want it to encompass all of death and all of death's secrets. But a floating image distracts me. An image that I want to imitate, to reproduce right there so that then, yes, my deep meditation will leave no secret unpenetrated.

It's the image of Hamlet beside the grave. No; it's the image, hanging on the wall at my parents' house, depicting Hamlet beside the grave.

In my attempt to imitate it, to make the picture — my picture — the same as that other one on the wall, I cannot penetrate a single deathly secret.

I only see Camila. I can only wonder who was in the right and who was wrong: Athens or Byzantium, Florence or Paris. I can only reach the conclusion that they were all wrong, and their error was caused by their universal ignorance of what the statue standing there before their eyes really represented. Then — ignorant, and wanting to displace their ignorance — they tried to approximate a random truth: Athens, Byzantium, Florence, Paris.

They were ignorant of the fact that this was Camila, my beloved, unfortunate Camila; that this was her little body, always so resistant to love, and today exposed to the eyes of all; that this was the fruit of my utter lack of responsibility, protected by a mortuary gravestone and made marble by murder.

A month of daily visits.

For the first twenty days I went alone. Starting on the twenty-first, Desiderius Longotoma kept me company.

By now, all the homogenous powder from his grinder machine had been absorbed into his pores, and the good man was starting to feel drawn to the dark calm of burial grounds.

"You will be my audience, Desiderius Longotoma. No hasty flattery! I want your honest, unpremeditated opinion, Desiderius Longotoma."

"All right, my friend, agreed."

This, night after night.

I take in my left hand a big, round lump of clay. Ever since that old lady's visit, I have been obsessed with hands holding lumps of clay. I stick an imaginary women's shoe into it. Not Camila's, no. I stick in the black patent shoe with a red heel that belongs to Lassette. Because I kiss Lassette, especially when she wears shoes like that. And since Camila never gave me her lips, now, using the image of Lassette's little heels, I kiss, mutely, she who is no longer of this world.

I reach a finger toward the statue, and, touching it, I exclaim, despondent and haughty, "Here hung those lips that I have kissed I know not how oft. Where are your gibes now? Your gambols? Your songs? Your flashes of merriment that were wont to set the table aroar?"

"Bravo, bravo!" Desiderius Longotoma manically shouts: "Now that's art!"

And he laughs, for Desiderius Longotoma usually shows enthusiasm by laughing. His sweet, cascading laughter rings out.

Then I, emboldened, "Not one now, to mock your own grinning? Quite chapfallen?"

I make a sweeping circular movement with my right hand, while the lump of clay falls and breaks, and the image of the little shoe, now belonging to both women, flies through the air. My tragicism peaks. I declaim, "Alas, poor Yorick!!"

Desiderius Longotoma, practically in ecstasy, "Magnificent, my friend, magnificent!"

And he laughs and laughs.

This, night after night, for ten nights.

And a third story begins.

Cirilo Collico is a painter. He is a distinguished, commendable painter. Though he does not and has never shown any audacity at all, though you can expect not a drop of innovation from him, there's no denying that he has a certain sweet, almost feminine sensibility, or at least something that everyone agrees — I don't know why — should be considered a feminine sensibility. Cirilo Collico enjoys soft colors: blue, violet, glaucous emerald. He spends long hours contemplating the blurred tonalities that time and rain deposit on pebbles. A canvas over half a meter in size frightens him. On sunny days he shuts himself inside his house. On freezing days he walks along the humble streets on the outskirts of town, leaving tears of emotion in the gray air. His ideal, his supreme ideal, is to someday paint the light of a diurnal flash of lightning. Nocturnal lighting makes his nerves bristle, and he hates it as much as he hates the Sun, Rembrandt, Dante; just as he detests firearms and the blood-red lips of women who hold one's gaze. On the other hand, alone in his workshop under the rainy skylight on a winter's noon, Cirilo Collico vibrates like a lute string when, all of a sudden, his walls light up for an instant with the hollow, washed-out green of a stray flash of lightning.

Cirilo Collico is a detective. He is a sharp, shrewd detective with the eyes of a lynx and the speed of a hare. In recent years, scarcely any scandal or crime has been cleared up without Cirilo Collico's involvement. When the police get a case without any leads to follow, one of their officers always comes to his workshop to ask for guidance. Cirilo Collico listens, takes notes, studies, sniffs about, goes out, runs around, questions, monitors, deduces, catches and finds.

Several days ago I was talking about this personage with Javier de Licantén, the great seer.

"How do you explain," I asked him, "such duality in a man? A refined painter, delicate like an almond, and also a passionate detective when it comes to wicked and bloody deeds."

"There is no duality," he replied. "Cirilo Collico is, has always been, and always will be a detective, nothing but a detective, and it is merely a certain sinful inner shame — when he realized that he was only interested in wicked, bloody deeds — that makes him sit in his wintry workshop and imitate a person as subtle and exquisite as almonds."

Not long after that I spoke of the same matter with Doctor Linderos, an eminent psychiatrist. To my question he replied, "There's no duality. Cirilo Collico is, has always been and will always be a very refined painter, and nothing more. And his fineness is so extreme, he is so refined and to ever greater extremes, that he has come to feel that if he keeps on in that vein, he will end up totally removed from reality, and he very much fears that. So, faced with this danger, he uses his moments of leisure to sink into said reality, as naked and cruel as he can find it — that is, full of blood and wickedness."

"Whatever the case," I said, "I'd like to know one thing, doctor: Why does Cirilo Collico insist on visiting me?"

"That, my friend," he replied, "you will find out soon, very soon."

And he walked away smiling.

* *

Yesterday I met with Cirilo Collico. We spent a long time strolling through the streets and talking about painting, only about painting. We didn't say a word about his detective work.

Amid the racket of passersby on calle del Zorro Azul, our path crossed that of Desiderius Longotoma, who was walking on the opposite sidewalk. When he saw me he put a finger to his temple, and then, laughing, he shouted, "Alas, poor Yorick!"

I blushed. Cirilo Collico stopped me. Then, with a thick accent, he asked, "What did that man just stay?"

I replied haltingly, "He's spouting nonsense, I don't know; I think he said: 'Alas, poor Yorick.' He's kind of a crazy guy, you know?"

Cirilo Collico, then, "I see."

A pause.

"Tonight you'll have news from me."

Another pause.

"For now, goodbye!"

And he walked slowly away.

Just as I was lighting my after-dinner cigarette, the doorbell rang. It was the mailman. He handed me a small envelope.

I opened it and read, "Cirilo Collico cordially greets his friend Juan Emar and humbly begs him to go to his father's house without delay, to pick up his top hat and look at what is inside."

I obeyed.

Minutes later, I was saying to Dad, "Where's your top hat?"

"Over there, on the dresser."

"May I look inside it?"

"My children can look at anything they want to in my house."

I walked over to it.

I looked.

Inside Dad's top hat there was nothing, absolutely nothing.

What kind of joke or foolishness, then, was that card from Cirilo Collico? When suddenly, my heart skipped a beat and I felt faint. Down in the bottom, printed on the silk lining, was the hatmaker's brand: above, its name; below, its address in London; in the center, Great Britain's coat of arms. That is what I was meant to see.

The British coat of arms has a crowned lion on one side; on the other . . . a magnificent and proud unicorn!

I didn't sleep last night.

Today, at cocktail hour, Cirilo Collico came over. We sat beside the fire. I called in my servant and was about to ask for whiskey. Then I thought it perhaps preferable to have something from another land; yes, from another land.

"Viterbo, two glasses of port please."

We drank in silence.

Suddenly Cirilo Collico said to me, "The Middle Ages were an extraordinary time."

"Certainly," I replied.

Another silence. A dog barked in the street. I called, "Two more glasses of port!"

Cirilo Collico drank. Cirilo Collico said, "Read of the misfortunes of Dragoberto II, sovereign prince of Carpadonia, back in 1261."

And he handed me a small, old, leather-bound book opened to page 40. I read:

"And so it was that Dragoberto II, drunk on blood, wanted to devastate as many lands as the hooves of his indomitable horse could tread. But upon crossing the peaks of the Truvarandos Mountains and entering the green Parpidano Valley, there suddenly appeared, holding the Redeemer's cross on high, the eldest of the monks of the Holy Brotherhood of the Unicorn, and . . ."

* *

My voice caught in my throat. I coughed. I shifted my feet.

"Damn!" cried Cirilo Collico, looking at his watch. "It's time to eat. I'm off, I'm off."

From the threshold he told me, "Tomorrow we'll continue with the reading. First thing tomorrow."

And he left.

As soon as the sound of his footsteps faded away, I fled my house like a madman. I ran and ran.

I reached the cemetery. I came to Camila. I prayed for one last time in my existence. This time, a scorpion and a pigeon were my chorus. Amen.

I raised the gravestone. And sweetly I lay down in my putrefying entrails.

Putrescences have a tendency to rise up toward the heavens.

Mine rise up with the speed of passing ages. They rise unstoppably. They rise through intra-atomic interstices, filling them as they go.

They've already passed through the coffin's lid. Now, the stone. Now they're touching the soles of Camila's little feet.

And they keep rising.

They flood Camila.

Camila is covered, from inside out, with my putrefactions.

Camila covers her idolized little body with a patina of tender, limpid pestilence.

Artists from the whole city contemplate her, enthralled.

One has said, "It's the patina of Paris."

Another has said, "It's the patina of Florence."

Another, "It's the patina of Byzantium."

Another, "It's the patina of Athens."

THREE WOMEN

Papusa

DIRECTLY FROM BEELZEBUB, AND DOWN THROUGH ALL of my ancestors in a straight line, an opal has come rolling. Long years ago it rolled down to me, as all my ancestors had gone to the grave and Beelzebub hasn't shown his face on Earth in ages.

When my father held it out to to me from his coffin, I reached through the candles all around him, and as soon as I felt him place the opal in my left hand, I covered it with my right to make sure none of that atmosphere of flowers and corpses got lodged in its iridescent twinkling and followed me home. I left the blazing chapel filled with deep emotion, slowly, and with a bowed head, weaving through the supplications of those who were praying for the deceased and the muffled sobbing of all the rest. When I got home I looked at the gem only for a moment, then tossed it into the drawer of my worktable. And there it has remained, as I said. Long years has this remote opal remained, its existence as idle as the ocean's.

But last night, fatigued from reading and meditation, I tore it from its glaucous idleness. I gazed upon it, and began to contemplate its profound and mysterious inner life.

Inside, the very great and very terrible Tsar Palaemon had set up his court, with his favorites, his minstrels and halberdiers, his footmen and harem, his gazelles and ghosts.

There reigned — there thundered — the righteous Tsar Palaemon, and as he reigned and thundered with his powerful silvery voice, inscrutable among four alabaster columns, the faithful Trabuchadnezzar, that herculean Black man in a tiger pelt, spun his scimitar which split the air into a sparking circle, like an echo.

Mute, seized by a thousand dark forebodings, I watched as a scene in that court unfolded slowly before my eyes, a scene as solemn as a sacred rite.

Tsar Palaemon thundered, and the silver of his voice pierced my eardrums while, down there, all fell palely silent. Trabuchadnezzar's scimitar scraped the air, and a wisp of freezing wind touched my face; down there, the red and black courtiers shrank back and fearfully hid within tall tapestries' faded gold, while the women's warm marble trembled, and the halberdiers bowed, and the gazelles fled in terror somewhere I couldn't see them. Only the ghosts didn't flinch. They stood, slender and graceful, beside their Lord and Master, their empty eye sockets staring straight ahead at the ermine curtains embroidered with topaz and garnet.

There was a moment of waiting.

Then, making the gemstones wink, a bishop emerged from the curtain's folds, an immense bishop with an infinite miter and a shepherd's crook that blazed like fire.

Another moment of waiting. Trabuchadnezzar's scimitar whistled through the air, footmen and minstrels cowered, and the silvered voice of the sainted Tsar Palaemon spoke to the bishop. "Release her!" he cried.

That was all. And there was a third moment of waiting.

The bishop lifted his robes that rose rustling from the floor, sank his hand in among the silks at his belly, and pulled out and shook and threw to the ground, before everyone's eyes, Papusa's soft body, with her bronze hair, her unheeding gaze, her breasts, her sex, and an imprecise smile that swayed for a long time.

The magnanimous Tsar Palaemon shouted, "Bring her to me!"

Then the sapphire diadems on the sole of an episcopal boot kicked and pinched Papusa's flesh.

Papusa gets up, walks forward.

She reaches the center. She stops.

The carpet is purple. The atmosphere, sea green. The light, slightly yellow.

And then came the fourth moment of waiting. No one moved. Only the ghosts trembled a bit.

Fourth moment of waiting, interminable. I wait like all the rest, like the pious Tsar Palaemon, like the very least of his buffoons.

And now I hear, I hear there in the watery distance, a dizzying distance that gets more and more dizzying the more desperately trapped it is inside the remote opal sphere, I hear something, something indefinite, and it gets louder.

It's the gazelles, fearless now, approaching.

They're galloping.

They smell, at any distance and through any terror, Papusa's bare skin.

She is their sister, alone there in the center, with thousands of eyes staring at her.

They arrive. They stand, rigid and fine.

They look. Their nostrils flare.

Tsar Palaemon flares his own. Everyone breathes and dilates. The bishop, the ghosts, the halberds.

Papusa has the hint of a smile.

And then comes a long moment of waiting.

I wait like all the rest, like the magnates and puppets. Those thousand dark forebodings have me in their clutches, gasping for air. I wait.

Papusa! My Papusa!

Tsar Palaemon straightens. His breastplate inflates and shrinks like a gigantic wave. His index finger points. His voice resounds: "You!"

A courtier advances, young, blond, with eyes oceanic like the air, dressed all in indigo.

On the carpet, Papusa lies down and opens. On the carpet, and also below my head, bent and heavy over the gem and my worktable.

The bishop blesses, raising his cape.

All eyes are fixed on the scene. All are calm, except for Tsar Palaemon.

Tsar Palaemon is restless, agitated, clattering the pearls and flowers hung from his throne. Then his eyes ask a question of his ghosts. The latter slowly shake their heads.

Tsar Palaemon's eyes ask, "Aren't we making progress?"

The ghosts' heads reply, "You are not making progress."

Then, as the courtier stands up, Tsar Palaemon cries out, "You!"

And this time his index finger points to a jester.

The feeble jester walks over, his green and saffron hunchback swaying.

Papusa falls.

The gazelles back up.

Papusa smiles vaguely, and her little smile sways sweet and pure, first enveloping the jester's body, then rising up through the air and out of the opal, and finally wandering over the walls of my room.

"Are we making progress?"

"No!"

What progress is the all-powerful Tsar Palaemon asking for? What do his ghosts see that they deny such progress?

I hold a loupe over the opal. I look intensely.

There I see, enormous, the jester's painted face. There I see the sadly divine, sadly smiling face of Papusa.

Nothing more.

Let's look some more. Let us look with all of our eyes, with our whole bodies, with all our blood. Those ghosts see something. Let us look.

I start to see.

There in the center, on the purple carpet, under the yellowish light, it's not just Papusa and the jester lying down. There's something else.

A coal-gray plume of smoke swirls around and surrounds the punchinello's forehead, nape, and temples; there is a small wheel of nacreous reveries starting to rise sweetly from Papusa's bronze tresses.

Both of them are thinking.

Let us keep looking.

I see, interwoven with the coal-gray smoke, the utmost pleasure that is given to man. The pleasure of the whole body. The pleasure of revenge, of vindication ... when one is deformed, monstrous, and beneath him lies beauty, adolescence — Papusa! I see a few of those bolts of maroon lightning shoot out from the coal smoke and strike the spectators, kindling a hunger, a fury, to possess. I see how all the thousands of beings there, all of them, form a single monster, just one, a monster with a hundred thousand heads but one single thought; with a hundred thousand hearts, but one single feeling; of a hundred thousand sexes, but one single lust ... Papusa!

Except for Tsar Palaemon, who trembles. Except for the ghosts, who silently despair.

Except the small wheel of nacreous reveries.

It rises up cleanly, not a single one of its atoms tarnished. Clear, distant, sublime. Just as it emerges from amid the bronze tresses, so it rises up, unchanged, constant, untouched, separate and pure.

Is Papusa utterly frigid? Not a shudder of pleasure ...; I understand that, yes. But neither a shudder of horror!

I slowly tear my eyes from the scene. I look toward the throne. There, hidden behind one of the alabaster columns, a ghost turns its hollow sockets toward me.

Then I ask, just as intently as I was staring a moment before, I ask.

And I sense what the ghost is saying: "Humans came into being without sex. Then sexes fell upon them, embedded themselves, and lived their own lives, feeding on the blood and ideas of humans. And so it was until today; so it is, now, always. Nearly eternal symbiosis that man refuses to recognize. Symbiosis that he no longer even feels. Abjectly accepted identification. There are some, however, who see, and at times even think. And sometimes, then, they sense that their sex lives for itself, sliding and dragging them — men, women, sovereigns — through caverns and revelations. In their arrogance they say: 'It is our will.' Wrong! They are dragged along. And there are others — rare exceptions — who know how things really are, they know, they feel and experience it. They have disconnected. They contain two separate lives in a being that only appears to be one. But they have broken the union, the pact, between human and sex ... as far as it can be broken today, on our Earth. Then the sex can go on living its own life forever, perhaps feeding on a little blood, but without preying on any ideas. Now, try to remember a distant occurrence, perhaps forgotten, but whose essence has remained in you, terrifying you every time life has offered you an analogous experience. Listen well: can you deny that an 'inexplicable' — because of the distance between cause and effect — dread catches hold of you every time you find life, out of nowhere, in that which you thought was inanimate?

"A very dark night in the countryside; there's a pile of stones, barely distinct, ghostlike. Then, in the pile, something moves, emerges, flees. A dog. But at first, perhaps one of the stones seemed to move; in any case, something you didn't expect to be alive. And you felt faint, you almost screamed. Life where you thought there was none!

"Years earlier. A movie theater. Circulating blood is projected on the screen. There they go, the flowing corpuscles. Slowly, something dawns on you: that stuff doesn't flow like a simple liquid, compact and propelled; it's alive in every particle, alive and free.

The corpuscles advance, stop, collide, form clumps, find their way, they search it out stubbornly and find it, and they speed along. Alive, every one of them, and living out their lives. Independent life adapted to the larger life! Adapted, yes, but independent. Inside you. You had to leave the theater.

"Dread that originates far back in your childhood, and now, when things that are in some way similar happen, they resound like an echo.

"Off on a childhood beach. A sea urchin's shell, already opened. You peer inside as if into the crucible of the world. Inside, black and wine-like liquid, blue ooze, the tongues of a seemingly blood-stained sex, all of it stirred up, destroyed by a knife, by cold steel. Scent of salty, cavernous seas; whiffs of pungent putrefaction. Suddenly, something in that inner cauldron stirs and lives on its own, reaching out six sharp, wet legs and wiggling them desperately. Just a little shrimp, the typical parasite of the urchin. But you didn't know that. And then a cry of dread: 'Mommy!'

"This dread was in turn a deeper and more distant echo. Dread born not, like the former, of a sudden instant, but slowly incubated by the stupefying life of the sex within you. Dread at the mystery of that sensitivity, that movement, which cannot be fully described as 'I'; which, fearful and disturbed, we call 'it.' Dread that — dozing, almost latent — remains by our side in life, causing us to vaguely ponder a strange duality, at times accepted, at others denied. Dread made pact. Permanent dread. Dread of what our destiny, thus coupled, must be.

"And from then on — as with all men, it must be said — you have experienced a sort of distrust of this intruder that governs, that can govern and subjugate as soon as it takes control of your true center of life, your IDEAS.

"You are doubting everything I'm telling you now. You doubt like all your peers who believe their presentiments, yet deny those same intuitions once they are confirmed. Doubt if you like. But first, put out your hand; move your fingers: look at them. See how that is you. Then see how you are you as well as it.

"Tsar Palaemon wants his subjects to adhere to the pact. Tsar Palaemon wants them all to remain on that confused threshold where they can sense a confused duality, but not to take one step further. Tsar Palaemon knows that as long as men are bound to such a pact, they are already virtually slaves, slaves to themselves, and, as such, easily enslaved by others, that is to say by Him, the just and magnanimous Tsar Palaemon. His iron hand, then, sinks into the sexes of his subjects, and that is why he rules, that's why he bellows, that's why he roars, that's why they tremble when faithful Black Trabuchadnezzar's scimitar tears through the air. Because there is no free man, woman, or gazelle in all his vast empire. The holy Tsar Palaemon knows all this.

"Until one morning, Papusa came before his throne.

"Papusa has disconnected. Her sex lives its life apart. Her ideas are left unscathed. Papusa is pure and free.

"Think now of what she represents, what she can come to represent in this vast empire: a being whose ideas cannot be constrained ... the beginning of freedom!

"Tsar Palaemon cannot bear such a thing. Tsar Palaemon has pinned all his hopes on a formidable trauma reintegrating Papusa's sex into her liberated personality. And in this way, once she is reintegrated, to sink in his hand, to manipulate, subdue, enslave, for the eternal, sublime glory of his powerful empire.

"A trauma ... That is why she is naked before the whole court. That is why the young man went to her. But it was not enough. That is also why the monstrous jester went to her, but that was also insufficient. Look at her smile of reverie. See how her ever more diaphanous thoughts rise up untouched. See how our Tsar Palaemon boils with rage at his impotence, his inability to bind Papusa's sex to her mind, to corrupt her, and, once she is corrupted, to subjugate her. Useless! Papusa is already freed, and no human force, even that of the Tsar himself, can subjugate her again to the curse that still holds sway over the rest of you.

"You thought of an abominable frigidity. Nothing of the sort! Look, in the nacreous reveries, see how there are long scarlet streaks.

"That is pleasure. Because she feels pleasure like every other being, just as you do, just as I felt pleasure when I was a man a thousand years ago. But even in pleasure, she is separate, she soars far above all the spasms, feeling them, yes, experiencing them, but without being them. That is why you see no shudders of pleasure, nor will you ever see a shudder of horror."

And the ghost fell silent.

Now the jester had risen and disappeared into the crowd. Tsar Palaemon, standing and brandishing his scepter, trembled. Papusa smiled vaguely.

I, bowed, bent, broken, almost embedded in the loupe, trembling as well, more than Tsar Palaemon himself, but from indignation, from a desperate desire to go to Papusa's aid and save her.

Tsar Palaemon shouts, "You!"

A footman takes two steps forward. The Tsar orders, "The dogs!!"

An expectant silence.

I hear in the far distance, a gallop. I hear it approach. They're barking. It's them. There they are!

Giant white mastiffs with black spots.

The same scene.

The whole court shudders. My loupe trembles so much that everything goes blurry and I cease to see.

The lens falls. I fall, and fall asleep.

Alone on the worktable lies the opal that, rolling, has descended from Beelzebub to me.

* *

Today I had it mounted in platinum and I wore it, along streets and in plazas, on my left ring finger.

Today, as soon as night fell, I looked intensely at it again. I called, "Papusa!"

There she is, alone.

"Papusa! Come! Leave that world of green and evil waters! Come to me! I don't care what the ghost says, get out of that hell-hole! Here there is love, peace! Come!"

Papusa smiles with her dear, vague eyes.

"Do you remember our past, our pure childhood, our love?" I asked her.

"Yes, I remember."

"So, you'll come?

"No. I am pure joy and above all, obedience. If you want me to come, let Him tell me, my Lord, the holy Tsar Palaemon."

Silence, long hours.

"Let Him tell me ..."

Why try? What interest could I hold, with my meager life and love, for the great and terrible Tsar Palaemon, whose reach extends beyond his subjects to his slaves and jesters, and beyond these to his dogs, and beyond his dogs, he must be surveying all of nature, seeking the way to make his whole Empire quiver with the tiny little wheel that spins out from my Papusa when her body goes down, down, down?

What interest could I hold, in the solitude of a shadowy, dusty bedroom, for her transparent reveries, her unattainable thoughts, which hold sway over an entire Empire and make it quake?

"Papusa! Give me some hope at least, just a little, just once!"

"If He wants it, then yes; if not, no."

* *

If not ... no.

No.

Tsar Palaemon has stolen Papusa from me, and I gain nothing by wearing his whole Empire on my ring finger.

Chuchezuma

ONE WINTER AFTERNOON IN THE YEAR OF 1932, I RE-
ceived a phone call from Luis Vargas Rosas, inviting me to his studio that evening. He wanted to show me his latest canvas, which at
the time he had not named but which I now call "Chuchezuma,"
though I don't know whether that name agrees with its creator.
To be sure, today the canvas is mine, which gives me certain rights
to name it as I see fit. And that's not all: the painting was already
partly mine, I think, even before it was made; it's just that I don't
know how to paint and Vargas Rosas does. Furthermore, when it
was painted, Chuchezuma had not yet played a part in my life,
even if all the threads of her destiny, as well as my own, were already leading us toward an inevitable meeting.

That night I ate in the small restaurant Au Petit Chez Soi, boulevard Pasteur. After coffee, I headed off to rue Belloni, where my
friend lives. Atop the building's low roof, I saw the illuminated
rectangle of his studio's skylight. On many afternoons and eve-
nings of ennui — of Parisian ennui, which is different from that
of all the other cities of the world — the light or darkness of that
rectangle has decided a portion of my fate, at least several hours
of it, which, what with the ennui — the Parisian kind — weigh as
much as several months' fate. Light indicates my friend's presence; that is, the evening is saved. Darkness means he is absent;
that is, I will drag myself through the streets, vaguely hoping for
something to happen. Now, it shines. A friend, a painting, a glass
of cognac, tobacco.

According to this logic of reactions, since the skylight was il-luminated, I should not have thought just then of the possibility of something happening. And yet, even as I saw the orange light amid the ash, I did sense something coming, and I crossed the street slowly so as to give my mind time to focus on that presenti-ment. I crossed. When I found myself at the front door, a woman walked past. A fine silhouette with a swaying walk, face hidden from the cold. She passed quickly. I followed her.

She was headed toward rue Falguière. When she reached it, she turned left. I hurried to catch up with her under a streetlight so I could see her. I saw her. She smiled. It was her — Chuchezuma!

I took her arm and we started slowly strolling. After a few pleas-antries, I pleaded with her for the tenth or twentieth time. And this time, to no small astonishment on my part, she consented. Our conversation went like this:

"Do you consent?"

"Yes."

"When?"

"Right now. If not now, never."

"Why?"

"Foolishness or a hunch, whatever you want to call it."

"Tell me more."

"I left my house thinking that something would happen to me. I almost think I believed that I'd belong to someone tonight, or never. And there you were. That's all there is to say."

All my astonishment vanished. Chuchezuma's words seemed to hold a fatal logic. I only had to remember, silently, my own presentiment at the illuminated skylight. That was all. And now, I believe, is a good time to provide Chuchezuma's biography.

She claims to descend directly from Montezuma. True or no? Perhaps she likes to play on the similarity of the last two syllables. We all tell her, "Light brown hair, white skin, green eyes. Don't lie."

She smiles and replies, "Many blond northern men have

splashed onto my lineage over the years, splashed on the long, long line of mothers with olive skin and warm-night eyes. Until I was born."

"You descend only from your forefathers, then."

"My face, yes; my body, no. It comes from olive groves, and its touch will bring nostalgia into any pleasure."

She smiles the whole time.

"And what do you do?"

"I love Mexico, I love Scandinavia, and I love France."

"That's all?"

"That's a lot for a woman ... and at my age."

"Certainly," we all reply.

She is seventeen.

And that is Chuchezuma's biography.

We walked on, still arm-in-arm. Moments later I proposed a small hotel in the neighborhood. She replied, "No. We're going to a different one. I'll take you."

That Chuchezuma knew of shady hotels managed to disturb me only for an instant. It was a detail that didn't fit with her biography. Plus, it was winter.

We went on arm-in-arm along rue Falguière, always headed toward the *fortifs*. After a few minutes we turned right into an alley I didn't know. It should be said, though, that I don't know that neighborhood well. The alley was calm; I would almost call it sweet. Then we turned again, this time to the left, into a narrow impasse. Just as calm, just as sweet. It all seemed like part of an uninhabited city. However, we could feel a vague heat coming off the cramped walls. Then, an old, austere gate. We went through. Now I was holding Chuchezuma by the waist. To my great surprise I saw that this gate did not lead to a courtyard, but to more alleys, extremely narrow and tortuous ones. Only the occasional light. Always the sweetness. Up above, between the barely perceptible rooftops, I saw a star. And that's all I'll say about the scenery. My sensation: a certain voluptuousness had been taking shape for some time, not just because of Chuchezuma's presence, but also due to the configuration of the streets and the slight bluish shade of the night. Then, after we crossed through the gate, there was a sudden increase in that voluptuousness, in which Chuchezuma's role remained always secondary. That is, the sexual aspect of the voluptuousness was minimal. Its essence was something else, which I could define as "irresponsibility." Irresponsibility manifested in the following way: feeling deeply within oneself — and by "within," I mean, I insist, in the chest and in the throat — that one could do anything, especially if it went against morals or the law, without punishment either from without — that is, from other men — or growing within one's conscience. It was total freedom. The freedom, for example, to enter any house, to rape, to murder, and to know the score would be settled elsewhere, far away, without your involvement. Even greater freedom: to jump off a balcony, to fall and not be destroyed; to cut open one's own belly with a dagger, peer at what's inside, and continue on with life just the same; to reach both hands into the flames of the gaslight, and, without feeling any pain at all, to sweetly savor how one can do this and other men cannot. I squeezed Chuchezuma's waist, hard.

It wasn't necessary to actually perform any of those actions. The feeling or certainty that they were possible was enough to penetrate my whole body and hit my chest and throat. Perhaps, if prolonged, I would have eventually needed to act. For example: to commit murder or leap from a balcony, a very high balcony, and, falling, to open my arms, turn my head around so gusts of air would hit my chest and throat. But for the moment I was within the realm of the unnecessary, and there I remained. For something happened that was outside of my control, and all these sensations were exchanged for another, single one: fear.

What happened was this: suddenly, between the pillars of a

small doorway, several little dogs appeared, yapping loudly. The dogs themselves, to be sure, could not intimidate me, since they were the size of a shoe, but their barking, I told myself, might attract some larger dog that would savage us mercilessly. I was utterly defenseless, and even if, upon seeing such a dog, I had started screaming: *au chien, au chien*!!, I think it would have been able to tear me to bits in an instant. Chuchezuma said to me, with a hint of mischief, "There aren't any big dogs around here."

I hadn't said a word. But Chuchezuma is as perceptive as Edgar Poe's friend, Auguste Dupin.

I thought it meet to defend myself. "I fear no dog, no matter how large."

"Large dogs at night evoke deep within you, so very deep inside that you can't detect it, but they evoke, I know, the garou wolf. And you fear the garou wolf, don't deny it, just as you fear Satan himself."

I do not advise anyone to wander alone through fields at night if said fields produce in one a feeling that is sharp in the clarity of its calm and sweetness, and if the night has a certain bluish shade. In such cases there is, if not the certainty, at least a high probability of finding oneself face-to-face with a garou wolf. And if one is not extremely serene, and if one does not have vast knowledge of the subject, the man will inevitably lose the struggle. The garou wolf, after tearing into the carotid with its teeth, will drink half its victim's blood, and, as it walks away satisfied, its inseparable companions, the black vampires, will fall onto the remains to drink the other half. The garou wolf is as large as most of its earthly peers, agile as a squirrel, with reddish fur and a gaze cold as steel, piercing as a stiletto. Bullets don't wound it unless they have previously undergone long and arduous consecrations. A dagger will pass harmlessly through it, unless equally consecrated. And the same can be said of the garou wolf's brother the black vampire, a vampire no less than a meter tall, with oily wings and gunpowder eyes. I say "brother," because here the kinship differs from that of the animal kingdom, where wolf and vampire are unrelated; the garou wolf and the vampire are related even more closely than a common wolf and a fox, or a common vampire and a bat. Let's proceed.

That a large dog evokes in me the garou wolf, and that I fear it ... Chuchezuma's nonsense! I went right up to that small doorway, went through it, and strode through the alleys to demonstrate my bravery. A long time passed. I glimpsed streetlights, and streets that led far away. I strode. A landscape of large trees, country houses, a stream went by — a view I never would have thought could exist in Paris. The gleam of bustling cafe windows went by. People, a lot of people. More solitude, more bustle, unsuspected corners. I walked, resolute and sure. Streets, people, streets, lights. A few silences. I arrived.

I live at number 55 on rue Marcadet. It's a small apartment that I share with my brother Pedro. Fourth floor. I went into our living room, flopped onto a couch, and thought.

This couch was upholstered in yellowish felt. Beside it was another in maroon felt. Across from it, one in twine-colored burlap, and behind that, one in blue brocade. To my right, a couch in dark burlap; above it, one in tapir leather, and above that, cretonne with scarlet flowers against a black background. To my right, three more were in a line: two that were also felt, one green, the other rat-gray, and one of horse leather dyed blue. Above this last, another made of purple brocade. Two hung from the ceiling on either side of the lamp: the first, cherry and yellow burlap; the second, multicolored Japanese cretonne. That was all the furniture in our living room.

My brother Pedro dreams of a vast house with vast salons, and, all along its shadowy walls, vast couches. His dream has a long way to go before it finds enough matter to exist and endure in life. His dream is as yet no more than thinking matter, and its whirlwind has managed to accumulate and convert into palpable matter only a few of the many nascent couches. These couches are the initial forms of a fetus. This room, like a womb, shelters the first palpitations of the fetus to come and it gives off an odor, sometimes moldy and other times fertile, like freshly watered grass. In the midst of it all, breathing: me.

My brother Pedro, awaiting the birth, spends his days in the kitchen trying to transmute the culinary arts into alchemical science. Then, for leisure, he goes out into the streets and peers at all the couches in the city. When his path crosses mine, he scoffs and treats me with quite haughty disdain. Aside from this, I don't think he has any other occupation.

I lay down on the yellow felt couch and I thought.

The garou wolf does not have what we could call a mental function or a will of its own, for such things require one to have been born as we men and other animals are born, that is, being fertilized by a male of our species inside the womb of a female idem, and being carried and birthed by her. Conversely, the garou wolf is born of the thought and will of a man who already exists and has fallen into a state of trance. This man must be saturated down to his very last cell by all the hatred for his fellow men that can be endured, and, once in that state, he must know that his hatred is not a part of him, but rather something separate that is supported by him, that takes shelter in him as in a freely offered temple. Then, when he falls into the trance, he is like a mute church locked against the night. When the church is deserted and silent, the God or Devil who inhabits it to feed off the prayers and brains of the faithful, peers out from its towers, flies through the air, meditates. And so with that Man's hatred. It peers out, it leaves, but, unlike the God or Devil of the church, it cannot find the strength to meditate, for the very reason that it is neither God nor Devil, but is limited to the human sphere. Then it feels disoriented, it longs for the mind of its master, and it wants to return there and induce action, and to guide this action with its intelligence. And it would return, if other beings did not intervene. For there are other beings whose bonds with humanity have been entirely severed, who are linked to humanity only by their ferocious hatred for it. But since they no longer have, as I say, any bonds, they cannot find the matter by which to excrete their hatred and empower it to inflict pain upon man. They now see something like a clot of hatred, so to speak, but out in the wilds and made of thinking human matter. That is, they see the possibility of reforming a bond. They pounce. Agile and wise as they are, they shape, they reify, they create that wolfish thing with reddish fur and steely gaze. Then they electrify it, they inspire it. And the wolf takes off like a flash to hunt and kill. Later, once it is satiated with human blood, these agile and wise beings disassemble the wolf, taking the blood for themselves and refining it along with the matter. Then the hatred returns to its human master, fortified by its long contact with blood. And the master awakens with all the voluptuousness of vengeance taken in the darkness.

Now let us look at the garou wolf's brother, the black vampire. The process is the same in all its parts save two: 1) The creator is not, as in the previous case, a man in a trance, but rather a man who is dead; 2) The agile and wise beings who reify and disassemble do not refine all the blood sucked by the black vampire, as they do with the garou wolf, but they leave a certain amount for the master or creator; that is, the dead man.

I will say a few words about these two points: there are men who have lived with so much hatred (and in this word "hatred" I synthesize all the baseness and ignominy of which modern man is capable), that, when they die, their thirst is still far from sated, no matter how many murders they have committed. As such, they need to remain connected to this life in order to continue their work of extermination, and they cannot resolve to set off on the pilgrimage that necessarily would take them further from the object of their hatred, that is, of their passion — which, I might add, is indomitable. A problem arises: the disintegration of their bodies fatally breaks all bonds and contacts with man, that is, all means of inflicting pain. They need, then, to preserve their bodies and keep them from disintegrating. The only way to do that is to continue infusing them, in their coffins, with human blood. That is why those agile and wise beings leave part of the spoils for the black vampire. Everyone benefits.

Ultimately, however, I am not writing a treatise about the black

vampire or the garou wolf. I only write about them because Chuchezuma's mischievousness evoked them in me, and only one fact about
them interests me: that in the world, in this world, in the night, in
these nights, there are beings — similar to us or different, I don't
care! — that act completely free of intelligence or a will of their own,
that act at the behest of other beings who take control over their disoriented state, over their passions that extend beyond their skin. That
is all that interests me. And let us continue.

I thought for a long time on the yellow felt couch. I thought until
my brother Pedro appeared on the threshold of our living room,
smiling and disdainful.

One look is all it takes for me to know his intentions: my
brother Pedro wanted me to tell him that it is highly absurd to
accumulate couches for a problematic future house full of vast
salons. When I do, he always finds the means to refute me and
demonstrate that whatever I do is even more absurd. And he dem-
onstrates it so clearly and with such disdain that, for a long time
now, I haven't said a word about his reprehensible couches.

This time, the man saw that he would be unable to pull me
from my silence. He said nothing about our living room's furniture. Only after several minutes did he speak, and it was about
his kitchen.

He said, "Would you like to have dinner tonight?"

"Depends what you're offering," I replied.

His answer was, "Come with me to the kitchen."

With his own two hands — so he said — my brother Pedro had
caught a magnificent lobster, promising enough to excite the most
exacting gourmand, and large enough to excite the biggest glut-
ton. Now he was preparing to kill it.

Then, with a certain undertone somewhere between saccha-
rine and mocking, which those reading this have not heard, certainly, and can't even imagine, but that for me is now and has
been for years a sort of recurrent calamity: "This, brother," (al-

ways brother, never my name) "is the great advantage of eating shellfish: you kill them yourself with no need for accomplices. This way, absorption and nutrition are perfected. Oh, to believe that only what is chewed and swallowed is food! Wrong, brother, wrong! According to my calculations, at least a third of the total nutrition comes from the edible being's agony and death. That's in terms of the — let's say — physical side of the matter. As for the moral side, let's return to those accomplices. Do you think it is fair to have another man killed so you can later appropriate the two-thirds of the spoils of his murder? Unfair, brother, unfair, my little brother! And, above all, cowardly. On the other hand, with these critters, the responsibility lies fully on oneself and no one else, which is befitting of a man. These creatures are wonderful things, and I respect them as they well deserve. There are others that are perhaps more respectable, although ... Maybe they're more respectable in a purely logical sense ... Well, we'll get to all that. In any case, an ox is intolerable and unattainable. Can you imagine one here, in this apartment?"

I couldn't help but chime in, "I don't know, Pedro, if it would be possible to bring an ox in here, what with the laws enforced by the police and the concierges, but yes, I can imagine it, of course I can! And not just one ox, but as many oxen as you have couches, with each ox lying on its own couch. I'll tell you: remember Luis Buñuel's film *The Golden Age*, with that cow in the girl's bed? Yes? Well then, ever since I saw that, I have only one obsession, I'll admit, just one hope: to someday see a cow or an ox — doesn't matter which — on every one of your couches. But go on with what you were saying."

Here, a smile that was contemptuous and above all gracious, extremely gracious.

"To hell with the likes of Buñuel and with you! The thing is that I, personally, am not about to slaughter an ox or even a pig. My scope is limited to a big lobster like this one. Well, a moment ago I was saying that there are other creatures perhaps superior to shellfish. I was referring to birds. A chicken, for instance. It's just the right size, no one will stop you from bringing it home, and then we just give its neck a squeeze. Not a milligram of the death-agony third is lost. But on the other hand, chickens do have, at least for me, a certain inconvenience. I'll explain: every edible being — and let me tell you, there are a lot more edible beings than people think; just ask any cannibal, or the folks who live on our mountaintops and come down in summer to hunt scorpions and kissing bugs that later they savor with delight on the long, silent, snowy nights — every edible being, I say, offers two kinds of sustenance: the solely physical one that, as you know, accounts for two-thirds of the total nutrition; and the other, let's call it the moral part, or better yet, the psychic one, which accounts for one-third. The first two thirds are chewed and swallowed, more or less seasoned, and any doctor or dental hygienist can give you plenty of information about their nutritional benefits. In my particular case, shellfish meat sits marvelously well with me. The last third, brother, is a different matter. Listen well: every being, during its agony and especially at the moment of its death, gives off, releases — I don't know how to explain it to you, who are profane, horribly ignorant in these matters — anyway, it gives off into the air a ... a ... how to explain it? You really are hideously ignorant. Let's say a double of itself. This double in essence carries inside it the moral qualities of the being to which it belonged in life, and these qualities are analogous, parallel, the exact reflection of its physical aspect. Oh, but this next part is a difficult point that I don't know if you'll ever be able to fathom! The point is this: knowing how to use physical qualities to determine a being's moral qualities, its essential characteristics, the prototype to which they belong, which they represent in principle — almost in an abstract principle, I'd say. No, you're not going to understand this, but it doesn't matter. For example, this lobster — what does it say to you? You will ask: what moral qualities does a lobster have? No, man! You see how you're on the wrong track from the very start? Don't ask anything, for God's sake! Look at it, just look! Look at it intently, ideally enlarging it in your imagination until it's the size of an elephant, or else shrinking yourself to the size of a flea. Then see its eyes bulging at the ends of gigantic stalks, see the crunching movement of its slow legs, see its half-waking cave-dwelling life under the armor of its shell, see the vague, muffled echoes in that foggy rudiment of consciousness, see its mouth, see its flexible tail with viscous slits, see — what the hell! — the mind that thought, that thought in such a way that its thought took the shapes you've been looking at. See that originating thought and intuit that, if this thought is truly roaming alone through our Earth's atmosphere, then, once incorporated, it impels another lobster to crawl laboriously between the underwater rocks. And you will see that every lobster is a monster, a terrifying monster from hell, though also peaceful and sad, and perhaps for that reason all the more tenacious. That's it, brother, that's it! So kill it, enjoy its agony and breathe it in deeply, not just through your nose but through every pore. All of it will nourish you. And then, yes, and only then, later, at your table surrounded by people who ideally are dressed for dinner, only then will you know how to taste its white flesh, why it's dripping with mayonnaise, why women, if they are young and beautiful, dart and narrow their eyes in a certain peculiar way as soon as that mayonnaise touches their tongues and their teeth crunch into the first piece of meat. But no! You are comically, ineffably ignorant, and so it is and will always be hopeless!"

And Pedro laughs heartily, he scorns me, crushes me, drags me down with his big squirming lobster in both hands.

What to do?

I knew that scoundrel would go on talking about the same thing for hours, and his voice and gestures had paralyzed me, robbed me of the strength to leave the kitchen. Until salvation arrived. My right hand came to rest on my jacket pocket, and I felt an object I suddenly recognized and remembered.

I found my lost strength. I said to Pedro, "I'll leave you to your lobsters and your nutritional theories. I think tonight I'll skip dinner. Thank you, but for now, I'm off!"

And I went back to our living room and lay down on a couch, this time the twine-colored burlap one. I decided, then, to meditate on, or better yet to savor, the sweet plans that the object would doubtless give rise to.

It was a little book of Paris maps by district, the kind they sell at all the kiosks and metro stations. Just moments ago, when we were going deeper into the alleys beyond rue Falguière, Chuchezuma had handed it to me, saying softly, "Hold this for me, will you? My bag is so full. But please don't forget to give it back when we part ways."

A promise on my part, and ... forgotten. Chuchezuma!

To hell with Pedro and the unfathomable voluptuousness of his lobsters! A lobster ... And I, on the other hand — Chuchezuma! It's true that the lobster agonizes and dies. And there is, as a result, the matter of the double, just as he says. It agonizes and dies ... Poor Pedro's lack of imagination! There can be agony and death and the release of the double, the originating and primary thought, into the air to be breathed in through the pores, there can be agony and death that is not the end, and then there can be rebirth and a new beginning. Chuchezuma!

I wanted to savor my plans while moving my fingertips over the streets of Chuchezuma's little map of Paris.

But in spite of my attempts, my mind, like an automaton, repeated the lines by Éliphas Lévi I had read a few months before in his *History of Magic*:

Physiognomists have observed that the majority of men have a certain facial resemblance to one or another animal. It may be a matter of imagination only, produced by the impression to which various physiognomies give rise, and revealing some prominent personal characteristics. A morose man is thus reminiscent of a bear, a hypocrite has the look of a cat, and so of the rest. These kinds of judgments are magnified in the imagination and exaggerated still further in dreams, when people who have affected us disagreeably during the waking state transform into animals and cause us to experience all the agonies of nightmare. Now, animals — as much as ourselves and more even than we — are under the rule of imagination, while they are devoid of that judgment by which we can check its errors. Hence they are affected towards us according to the sympathies or antipathies which are excited by our own magnetism. They are, moreover, unconscious of that which underlies the human form and they regard us only as other animals by whom they are dominated, the dog taking his master for a dog more perfect than himself. The secret of dominion over animals lies in the management of this instinct. We have seen a famous tamer of wild beasts fascinate his lions by exhibiting a terrible countenance and acting himself as if he were a lion enraged. Here is a literal application of the popular proverb which tells us to howl with the wolves and bleat with the sheep. It must also be realized that every animal form manifests a particular instinct, aptitude or vice. If we suffer the character of the beast to predominate within us, we shall tend to assume its external guise in an ever-increasing degree and shall even come to impress its perfect image on the Astral Light; more even than this, when we fall into dreams or ecstasy, we shall see ourselves as ecstatics and somnambulists would see us and as we must appear undoubtedly in the eyes of animals. Let it happen in such cases that reason be extinguished, that persistent dreams change into madness, and we shall be turned into beasts like Nebuchadnezzar. This explains those stories of garou wolves, some of which have been legally established. The facts were beyond dispute, but the witnesses were not less hallucinated than the garou wolves themselves.

To be sure, that's how these stories are explained. A pungent and captivating scent had spread through the air. Pedro had poured several drops of wolfsbane extract into the boiling water he would use to kill the lobster. From whence the perfume.

"WOLFSBANE (*Aconitum napellus*). Profane amateurs should not use this plant for medicinal purposes, as it carries serious risks. *Occult botanics*: Lives in cold, dry environments. The plant is used (mixed with rue, saffron, and aloes) in fumigations to ward off evil spirits. It is one of the Rosicrucians' twelve plants. According to the Greeks, it sprouted from the saliva of Cerberus when Hercules pulled him from hell. It is also thought to regrow hair. Planet: *Saturn*. Zodiac sign: *Capricorn*."

Rodolfo Putz — *Magical Plants*

Now came the sound of the frenzied, desperate struggle of the poor victim boiling in water, in water heated, thanks to the wolfsbane, to above one hundred degrees. I could hear Pedro's breathing, rhythmic and deep.

I left.

I was absolutely certain that in a few minutes I would find Chuchezuma. I left. I cleared out.

The orange rectangle of the door of a bar. There, leaning slightly out toward the street, Chuchezuma. Now she was dressed in fiery red.

I approached the door and took a look inside. It was a tavern — a bar, if you will — all painted green. At the counter, leaning on his right elbow, a man was drinking a glass of cognac.

That man could well be Chuchezuma's lover, or in any case, the reason for her wardrobe change. Over in Belloni-Falguière, I forgot to mention, she'd been wearing dark gray. So, then, I took precautions to keep from being seen. I pressed my back to the wall, as though to embed myself in it. From this position, all I could see of the bar was a long, narrow, vertical strip through the angle of the doorway. I couldn't see the man. But a light behind him cast his shadow onto the wall that, in said strip, I could partially see. And so, from there, I could glimpse the tip of a hat, the tip of his nose and tie, all in shadowy green and enlarged to gigantic proportions, up high, very high, almost by the ceiling.

Then I remembered the question of another date between Chuchezuma and me. As I recalled ... let's see: I think, yes, it was to be Wednesday at five in the evening. I handed her the map, which she took quickly and covertly. In a very low voice, then, so the guy inside couldn't hear, I asked, "Wednesday at five, you said?"

She replied, in a loud, resonant voice, "Yes, Wednesday at five, they said."

And she left the doorway and walked off down the street, down all the streets of Paris ... that's how it felt when she walked away like that.

Alone again, on this side of the door. Between my desires and her disappearance there are still the eyes of that man who, if I move forward, will catch sight of me when I step into the orange light spilling onto the sidewalk. He will know I am his rival, he'll come out, pounce on me, beat me, dismember me, kill me. So I stay, then, embedded in the wall, I stay there, I meditate, love, and tremble. I rhythmically inhale the Paris streets that swallow her, savoring her, filled with delight. I meditate. Chuchezuma!

She has devilish skill. She tricks and toys with any guy in any bar. She can do it all, just by changing the subject of a verb. I had asked her: "Wednesday at five, *you said*?" And she had responded: "Wednesday at five, THEY SAID." She can do it all.

Let's start with the assumption that the man in question had a very sensitive ear, or else — and this is more likely — I didn't have complete control over of my voice, and though I believed I had spoken very low, I'd actually spoken loud enough for him or anyone else in his place to hear me. The consequences aren't hard to guess : notice, come out, beat, dismember, kill. And Chuchezuma is watching out for my safety. When I said, "you said," it was one person, only one — since mine was the only voice — who was asking, and "you said" means that only one person must likewise answer, signifying a date between two people: he who spoke (me) and she who answered (her). And she is seventeen, dressed in burning red, with light brown hair, white skin, green eyes ... Guessable consequences. On the other hand, "they said ..." THEY

SAID means several people, many people who will meet on Wednesday at five in the evening. An *outing*, a group: no danger to her light brown hair. The guy can only go on drinking his cognac in peace. Let's check: he went on peacefully drinking his cognac, she was able to walk away down all the Paris streets, I — carefree — could meditate embedded in the wall. Chuchezuma can do anything just by changing the subject of a verb.

Peace. Let us meditate.

There is no more danger. The guy thinks only of his drink and does not see me as a rival. But if not for her guile, there would have been blood. Blood! Everyone, always, craves blood. In vain do we pretend otherwise and deceive ourselves: we want to feed on blood. The garou wolf and the black vampire are our brothers, and there's no hypocrisy involved. The garou wolf and the black vampire are our highest, though unconfessed, aspiration. The first verb of our conscious minds is "suck." I'd like to see Chuchezuma play with this verb just as she played with "say" a moment ago. The only vital color is red, the color she is wearing now, the color the grass or the roads or the streams are dyed when one manages to kill a garou wolf or a black vampire, spilling the blood they have sucked. Then … on your knees! On the ground! And resuck that once-sucked blood.

But who can ensure victory in such a battle? One needs — as I've said — weapons that have been lengthily, laboriously consecrated. Plus, you have to master a vast range of sciences.

Guile is better, stealthy guile. What I mean is this: instead of attacking these entities, seek, stealthily, their origin. You already know that behind each one is a man, either in ecstasy or in a coffin. Look for them.

Then, strike, strike mercilessly. The sympathetic echoes of your blows will fall upon wolf or vampire, and such blows they cannot bear. They will return to their original condition of cursed, immaterial will. And the blood they have sucked will spill out with a splash and form a great puddle. You know the rest: knees! forehead to the ground! suck!

Chuchezuma must be far away by now, a little way down all the streets of Paris. The bar had closed, the guy was gone, and no orangish stripe tinged the sidewalk. I can move forward now. I can walk like her, a little way down all the streets of Paris simultaneously. Vaguely. Chuchezuma will turn up.

I walked on.

All the vagueness gradually dissipated. A certainty set in. No, not all the streets of Paris, no: just one, a hard one. On it, a house rose above the rest, just one empty house.

At this idea — this certainty — something struck me mercilessly about the chest and throat: a childhood dream I'd always had was finally going to come true! A house, a big one, seven floors, at night, *empty*! A house like that: to go in!

I walked on.

Here it is: a solitary street, hard and asleep. Here it is: that's the house.

All its window blinds are open wide. None of the windows have curtains. All the windows are closed. That is, there is darkness in all the rooms, great darkness.

Somewhere in there, Chuchezuma.

I went in.

Not a rug, not a stick of furniture. My footsteps on the stairs echo up to the highest ceiling, strike there, and bounce back down as an echo. They rebound downward.

Now, all the rooms to myself. I can go in, slam the doors, stomp my feet, shout! Chuchezuma is in here somewhere.

I can even risk peering out through any random window at the street, inspiring fear, even terror, in some passerby. And if that passerby has — as is most likely — read Dostoyevsky and still trembles, he will remember the idiot prince, thinking that from the street he has seen, in the window of a big house, for an instant, Rogozhin's head. He will tremble at my head. I will back up quickly toward the opposite wall. I'll keep still, still! And his trembling will tremble in me ... Chuchezuma could be in any corner!

Another room. I can go in. Silently now. Not a sound, not even from my own footsteps. That way, the glaucous rectangle of the window stands out even more. And as I have read and trembled with Dostoyevsky (mentally, I mean, without ever stirring the air), like Raskolnikov in the old pawnbroker's room when "a huge, round, copper-red Moon looked in at the windows," I can think: "It's the Moon that makes it so still, weaving some mystery."

There is no Moon here, but there is Raskolnikov's dream. And the silence created not by the Moon, but by everything, by the wooden floorboards, the low ceilings, the half-open doors, by Chuchezuma's breathing, which makes no sound, but is in some corner of the empty house, somewhere!

I know I only have to walk decisively — that's it, decisively — in order to find myself face-to-face with her. And so, we will do nothing decisively. We will keep floating like this, in the darkness, making sounds, a knock, a whistle, setting each one off to run through all the house's nooks and crannies at the same time, upstairs, downstairs, everywhere at the same time just as Chuchezuma did a moment ago along all the streets of Paris.

The noises will pass through her, each noise will pierce her. I knock with my hands, stomp my feet, I whistle and sing.

I've taken out my gold watch, heavy and old, and thrown it into the air, and it fell, it shattered: each little cog, each spring, each screw and shard of broken glass, each little number on the face, has made its own particular sound, has moved through every intersection in the house, has crossed it, has perforated Chuchezuma, and in every sound, me.

Let us wait, let us wait, given that all it takes to find her is a decisive advance. We shall delay the moment. Think of her pale skin and young blood.

We do not drive our own thoughts. All of my will is seeking the power to manipulate that white skin and that blood. But the blood separates, leaves Chuchezuma, comes to present itself alone before me and make me think.

I feel it like a spurt, tall and motionless, here in front of me. I feel as though I'm on the threshold of a temple.

Enter it. With unction, enter and be drenched.

I'm in front of it, just on the threshold. I remain outside. I am filled only by that which whispers around it, like birds around the towers of a cathedral. That which agonizes, dies, spills blood, that which devours and sucks.

Right now Pedro is dismembering something, surely. In the fields, the wolves must be galloping and the vampires flying. How many defenseless men will fall! For there are very few who, upon crossing paths with one, can escape unharmed. Still, there are a few. They are those who have made use of an antidote against those beasts. The most recommended of which are:

Against the garou wolf: If its progenitor is of the masculine sex, that is, a warlock, take some finely ground black nightshade seeds, which have first been steeped in an infusion of myrtle, and add them to its food on the sly. This food will cause the subject's hands to erupt in small sores, which will bleed profusely. The subject will wipe the blood on a handkerchief. Steal that and soak it in pure water. This water will be dyed by the blood. Then mix it with wine and drink it all down. No garou wolf born of a warlock will attack anyone who has drunk of this wine.

If its progenitor is of the feminine sex, that is, a witch, there is no need to employ black nightshade, as it is enough to take possession of one of its monthly cloths and proceed as with the handkerchief above. Once this wine has been consumed, no garou wolf born of a witch will dare attack.

Against the black vampire: The same measure for both sexes. Find the coffin and open it. It will be full of liquid and fresh-looking blood in which floats the cadaver — if we can call it that — of the warlock or witch. Fill a small bottle with this blood, and then let the blood congeal. Grind up those clots. Use the powder obtained to make cookies in the usual way. Once these have been eaten, no black vampire will dare attempt an attack.

That's all, of the most recommendable methods, at least.

I will not be able to escape this cycle of thought. When thinking is impossible, it's better to act. Let us be decisive. Here on the upper floor there must be a vast hall, as long as the whole front of the building.

I go up. I enter.

There, across the room, Chuchezuma is standing with her back against the wall. She rests the palms of her two little hands on it. She smiles. Says, "I was waiting for you."

And she is silent.

I run to her.

I fall to my knees.

I embrace her legs and kiss her, I kiss her passionately. I can hardly breathe. I kiss her until, through the windows, dawn appears.

Chuchezuma leaves. I stay a few minutes longer to calmly smoke a cigarette. A ray of sunlight enters. I leave in turn.

Rue Belloni.

I immediately recognize the canvas that Vargas Rosas wanted to show me. It's exact. I tell him, "It's my favorite out of everything you've painted."

He says, "I thought you'd like it. Consider it a gift."

And here I have the canvas, silent and alive.

I haven't seen Chuchezuma again.

Lassette

IT WASN'T MY CHOICE THAT SENT US OFF TO VISIT THE mountains, and it wasn't hers. It was mere chance. We were walking along twilit streets, sighing with boredom and not speaking. My foot came upon a crumpled sheet of pink paper. I went on kicking it in front of me for a long time, forcing it to precede us in our march. Sometimes she was the one who kicked it. She was named Lassette, because she's very young. She has a slender waist and she doesn't talk when I'm not talking. But I know she is always with me. Proof: when one of my kicks launched the pink paper into her path, she punted it back into mine. When she did, the pearl-gray silk of her suit trembled, and beneath it breathed the beige silk of her legs. Finally, I turned a blind eye to her silks. The paper, having come so far with us, obliged us to take it into consideration. I picked it up and we read. It was a permit to visit the mountains. At the bottom it said, *Valid today only.*

Finally! Something new, something with which to fill a hole in life! Something more: something that was not this eternal stroll through these streets that dull our eyes to the point of darkness.

"Shall we go, Lassette?"

Lassette lowered her eyes and trembled. Lassette always trembles when I suggest we go somewhere. Go. Lassette has concentrated all her voluptuousness in the verb "to go." Doesn't matter where to. It's the act of going, and it's enough for her.

"Let's go," she whispered.

Then I looked at her with great care from head to toe. And

she wasn't trembling all at once, no. She trembled little by little, part by body part, gradually, while the rest of her being remained motionless, and so on in each part, each fragment, exactly where my two rays of sight landed.

We went to the mountains. We walked through galleries of snow tinged vaguely greenish by the constant twilight. Soon we reached an immense, flat expanse. We paused. Behind us, the night paused. There we stood in the green snowy twilight. Ten paces behind us, the sea-blue night waited in silence, standing still beside the sleeping peaks. In front of us and below stretched infinite layers of afternoon mountains, desperately — and I think suicidally, were I forced to walk them all — infinite. But in the background, at the very end, standing over those dead layers, extended another mountain range, solitary, rippling, brittle, blinking red and orange above stagnant clouds.

"It seems to me," I told her, "that there is something artificial in all of this, Lassette. Don't you think? The night isn't progressing. (It's true that we aren't either.) The twilight continues. (Certainly, us too.) The sun isn't moving toward the end of the mountain range. (It's true that we're right here, and we're not moving.) But how much can this really explain? I sense there's something artificial in all this, my Lassette!"

She said to me, "Let's go."

I don't know if she said it out of caution or just to conjugate the verb "to go" at me. She turned around and started to walk. Then I was gripped by an uncontrollable excitement. I ran to her. With my left arm I grabbed her around the waist from behind; with my right hand I lifted her skirts of pearl-gray silk. And since she was facing the night, that is, with her back to the fiery mountains, the fire reflected onto her flesh, now gilded and bloodied. I wanted to possess her gold and her mountainous blood. But Lassette slipped away, let out a bell-like laugh — she who never laughs — and ran off like a young animal.

I've always been more of a runner than Lassette. I can catch up with her anywhere, in any circumstances. And then I kiss her. Lassette is agile, she's a squirrel, deep down she is a kite, in the way she unravels and extends her life. But when we run she doesn't know what to do with so much young life, and I catch up with her, grab her, squeeze and kiss her.

Lassette took off running after my attempt to possess her by her sun. Bells tinkled as she ran and laughed, and I, my eyes filled with red and yellow, started to notice that it was hard, very hard to make my feet glide quickly over the green snow. I was barely advancing. I moved my legs as fast as possible, but even so, the ground did not slide beneath me in compensation for my efforts. And Lassette ran further away as her laughter bounced off the mute peaks.

I don't know if anyone will understand just how painful it is when each stride you take does not push enough ground back toward the abysses behind. I don't know. I for one suffered desperately. I suffered backwards, because of how little the world receded; and forwards, because of the growing immensity Lassette put between us. And what mortified me the most, with a mortification that drove me to deny God Almighty himself, was that the snow had nothing to do with that heavy slowness of my legs, nothing, nothing. It was a growing slowness, a slowness without reason or snow.

My poor Lassette! Amid all the youth of her laughter she must have noticed the dark spot of my pain at being unable to run faster than her, so as to catch up with her, fling her down, and perforate her, burning my sex in the flames of her flesh, flames stolen from the last of all the mountain ranges.

For Lassette stopped.

And then I devoured the distance between us in the briefest of instants. I understood then that it was Lassette's velocity, not an irrationality of my efforts nor of the universe's, that had slowed my own speed. I remained, then, at peace with all creation, I bowed down silently and fervently before Almighty God, and I said to Lassette: "Lassette, I love you."

Then Lassette slowly began to descend the spiral staircase.

Again, fear assailed me. Going down, that error of velocities could happen again. But Lassette had foreseen everything. Lassette bifurcated, she split in two. Two girls with watery youth, dressed in clingy pearl gray. One of them turned around the spiral, not very fast, no, but with such regularity, such constancy, with such totality, that never, ever could I have reached her side. The other one was slowness personified. She paused life itself for a second on each step, as she reached out a little satin foot and skimmed it over the next step. Thus she descended. And as she descended she hummed a slightly sentimental song.

I tried a second time with this second, lagging Lassette. Again I grabbed her from behind, lifted her pearl-gray skirts and saw her flesh that, shadowed now by the first flights of the spiral staircase, was also of bluish pearl. Then I possessed her. When she felt it, she turned her head around and we kissed, while the other one, slow, very slow, kept going down, the first Lassette now humming the song that this second one had left hanging because of the pain at first, and then the flood of pleasure. I possessed her with my eyes closed, but soon I opened them so I could also have her with my eyes, my Lassette. But when I saw her I realized with astonishment that she was changing, transforming, and that I was taking with all my extremities a woman I did not know. But it was too late, there was no force that could stop me, and, though she was unknown, I had to empty myself into this stranger that Lassette, in her silken detachment, had sown in the midst of my impotent chase.

For an instant the mountains and heavens were erased and total silence fell. Then I moaned, and awoke a moan from her, and, with our vibration, the mountains settled in again, the heavens were suspended anew, and Lassette's song climbed back up the spiral.

"Let's go down," the other woman said.

A hundred more steps down. Lassette was waiting for us, and when she saw us she smiled. Her smile held no irony, no pity, no resentment, nothing. It was a smile alone, isolated in the world. Then the three of us went on turning without talking.

Suddenly, a sound reached our ears: the steady echo of powerful steps as they ascended confidently. I felt an immediate and horrible fear. The climber was, I could tell from the sound of those footsteps, that man.

"So what?" I asked myself instinctively, like a protective flinch before a punch.

That pink paper, the visiting permit, flitted through my mind. But that memory was scuttled by a vague sense of unease. Of course I had the permit to visit, I had it right here. Still, I couldn't reassure myself. There was something else that would outweigh any permit, valid as it may be, to this man. Something wasn't right, something hadn't been right all along. I could feel it. He was surely going to find out, if he didn't know already and was climbing the stairs for that very reason. Something bad. And what most daunted me, what made that moment into one of anguish, was the vagueness of that evil. I ought to have pinned it all on the recent possession, especially because the woman was not mine. But no. That possession was neither for better nor for worse. What could it matter to that man? It mattered nothing to me. Nor to the woman, given that she had left it behind on the stairs. So what could it matter to him?

It was the sum total that wasn't right, that was somewhat off-kilter, or rather gave off a whiff — though very faint, it's true — of impending decomposition, or in any case of premature decrepitude. Above all, it was the existence of that mountain range we were leaving above, behind. None of that totality was located in the precise spot where everything can be forgiven and allowed to keep moving. But, what blame did I have in such things? Rigorous reasoning would respond: none at all. But less rigorous reasoning would be unable to overlook the fact of the simultaneity of existence — even if only in that moment in which I lived — shared by the mountain range, the sky, the stairs. Lassette, the other woman, and me. No one, then, who wanted to distribute blame and responsibility would ultimately absolve me. They would simply say, "If you are not in this whole thing at all, how is it that you are, precisely, in all of it?"

And the truth was that the ascending man's footsteps were getting closer.

I saw the tip of the crown of his big Mexican sombrero turn at my feet and disappear as he approached. I just had time to grab Lassette's arm and push her behind me. We hid between two pillars. If the man didn't think to look to his right, we would be free. Otherwise he would see us, and, on seeing us, his surprise would be matched by his fury. The other woman was in front of us, in the middle of the stairs, unmoving.

And the man appeared. With the same movement I'd made a moment before to grab Lassette, he grabbed the other's arm and roughly pushed her into a narrow gallery that led off the spiral staircase, crossing its axis and fading into the shadows. They both disappeared.

Then I whispered to Lassette, "Run!"

And we started to tumble down the stairs. The echo of our hurried steps must have been audible in the most distant reaches, because just then, a powerful voice reached us: "Oh, oh! Is it you two? Wait!"

And we heard that man, in turn, start to tumble.

As I said before, I have always been more of a runner than Lassette. Now, for every turn she took around the spiral, I took at least two, so that when she reached the foot of the stairs, I had already crossed the long hall and was turning into the foyer, lunging at the door to open it. First I removed a chain, then turned two locks and was about to pick up the key, when an explosion rang out in the hallway behind me. I began to move even faster. The shot had not yet fully died away when I flung the door wide open and again saw the calm, coffee-colored streets of my city. Then I called to Lassette, "Lassette! Lassette! Take heart! We're safe!"

I waited, trembling. Nothing. No one. Silence.

Suddenly Lassette appeared in the corner of the foyer.

She was walking with majestic slowness and her face was fixed in an expression of detached reflection. Her right hand swung like a pendulum to the beat of her calm steps. Her left hand rested on her waist.

When she reached me, she held that hand out to me. Blood dripped from it. Then I saw that starting at her waist, at the exact point where her hand had been before, her whole torso was turning red, quickly upward like a glass being filled, downward like a glass spilling. And so the red of her blood swallowed up the pearl gray of her silks.

I waited a moment. Nothing. I thought that the blood must have stilled, that its mission had been only to soak Lassette's dress, because her neck did not turn red, the beige of her stockings remained immaculate, and the black of her little shoes was still black like two coals on tiptoe.

But all of a sudden the heels of her shoes — just the two heels — went bloodshot, turned scarlet, and as the color sank to the ground the very earth around those two bases, in a tiny area, blushed slightly. Then I understood that the evil flowed within.

Filled with indignation, I began to shout as loud as I could to rile up the people against the wretch who had fired on Lassette, wounding and covering her in blood. We were now in the middle of the street. From all the neighboring doors came men, women, and children. I even saw an elderly man in the crowd. I cried, "The man over there tried to murder her! That man there, there!"

And I pointed to the door that was still open.

I could tell that indignation was washing over all those people. With a muffled, growing murmur, hardly moving their feet, they shuffled over to besiege the dark hole of the doorway. But when they were no more than two or three meters away, there on the threshold, to my great astonishment, that man issued forth against the black void.

And here I thought he'd be fleeing up the spiral stairs to escape the inevitable punishment for his ignominious act ...! No. He was right there, standing on the threshold. He was wearing a small bowler hat now, but he still had his high riding boots. He looked at no one. From his precipice, slowly, he looked toward me.

"They're going to tear him limb from limb," I thought.

I yelled, "That's the wretch there!"

Everyone looked at him with enraged eyes, fists clenched, ready to lunge at his throat.

"That's him!" I shouted again.

He stared at me the whole time. But the others didn't move. Perhaps they were waiting for him to provoke them more directly. For Lassette's wound was not a direct provocation for them, only for me. Lassette's wound was to them an abstract wound, a notion of a wound that angered them, certainly, but that floated in the air without driving into their flesh and muscle. That's how I thought of it. The other man stayed motionless and looked at me. I kept shouting, inciting them, my finger pointed straight at him. The people hesitated, and, little by little, their fists unclenched. Then, seeing the persistence of his gaze, they slowly turned their faces on me, and all those eyes questioned me.

I summoned all my strength and shouted, "Murderer!"

Just as slowly, all the heads turned to follow the trajectory of my cry, and their eyes, once again, landed on him. But I saw that the fury had left them, replaced by stunned interrogation. And since the other man didn't move, didn't blink, didn't breathe, for a second time the thousand eyes abandoned him and joined in with his gaze, falling and intercepting a second insult against that wretch before it left my mouth.

A sinister — to me — idea must have started to form in those people's minds: if all the guilt lay only with that man, he wouldn't simply stand there motionless, mute, and gazing at me with growing reproach. Then I tried, desperately waving my arms, to formulate a third aspersion, since the second had rolled down to my feet without anyone hearing it, except for the whole length of my own body. But I felt I had lost ground, that somewhere, in some remote, uncharted place, that man was at least partly in the right, and the rabble instinctively knew it.

A vague feeling of guilt made me go pale. No aspersion was heard. But my eyes cast a look of such anguish that everyone, yet again, turned toward the man, curious to see its effect on him.

Everyone looked at him, including me, and we waited. Then he made his first move: coldly and calmly he reached back, took hold of his revolver, and, even more calmly, pointed its muzzle at me, moving it from my feet to my head. All eyes followed the weapon and then looked my way to watch me fall. In that instant, I felt my blood seeping from my skin. It was green, like the dead part of the mountains we had just visited, like the flesh of the other woman when she was shadowed by the spiral staircase. And I saw my last hope, nested in the tip of my head, slip away and abandon me, flying like a frightened bird.

But just then, striding confidently with both thumbs hooked in his belt, a policeman appeared. He stopped in the middle of the scene. First, he considered the man with his gun still aimed at me, and, holding up his right hand with its palm open, he said: "Stop right there!" Then he considered Lassette and me, and with his other hand, like someone sweeping up garbage, he signaled that we should move along as fast as possible. The man obeyed; lowering his gun and putting it away, he gave a deep sigh, turned on his heels, and went back in through the door. We obeyed, too. Lassette and I slipped along the streets in a hurry. The crowd began to melt away. And the policeman took his leave.

"Lassette," I said to her then, "reason was entirely on our side. And for that very reason let us flee, so that those people may never see us again. For, with one bullet, with a single look from their still eyes, they can undo all reason, no matter how just."

After an hour we were in front of my house. I left Lassette, went inside, and ran to the basement. The basement of my house has a little window at the level of the sidewalk. I rushed over to it to see Lassette's footsteps go by.

They went by.

I saw her beige stockings, her satin feet, and her two sharp heels bathed in scarlet blood.

TWO PLACES

The Hotel Mac Quice

WE LEFT OUR ROOM, MY WIFE AND I, AROUND SUN-down. From there we went down a narrow hallway to the long gallery, wide and tall. This gallery was above all long. Its end was dubious. Its color was mainly yellow ochre. The marble columns, half inset into the walls, were of a slightly lighter ochre. The wall panels between them were almost brown, edged with a strip of gold; a second strip of edging, along the columns, was a chocolate shade. Gold predominated on the ceiling, but an old gold — very old. The carpet was tobacco colored. Occasionally, to the right or to the left, maroon draperies hung from the walls. Only once, an emerald-green hanging. The sum total of all I've described was, as I mentioned, yellow ochre.

But let us return to the carpet. It was, I repeat, the color of tobacco — a light tobacco, I forgot to say. This was not the most striking thing about it. The most striking thing was, without a doubt, its thickness. Of course there was no way to measure that, because the carpet reached all the way to the base of the walls on either side. But you could tell by its softness, and above all by its perfect silence.

Both my wife and I, as well as the bellhop who went ahead with our suitcases, walked over it with a very slow, pendular rhythm. Something else I forgot: the bellboy wore a cherry color, my wife wore the shade of ram's wool, and I the color of a crocodile that had been dead for days. My hat was of a malt-extract shade, my wife's was the color of burnt cotton, and the bellboy's was a hue of paper moistened with salt water.

But let us return to our gait. Since I compared it to the movement of a pendulum, I must add that this pendulum would swing backwards and forwards in relation to our bodies, i.e., in the direction we were walking; by no means would it swing from one side to the other, by no means like a scale; in sum, not at all like a bird flying over the rocks and away.

Keeping the aforementioned well in mind, this movement could be compared — though distantly, and, I repeat, without forgetting what I said above — to movements of Italian actors in their mediocre operas, most especially when they dress in fifteenth-century style, and even more so if they wear two differently colored socks, and one of them has vertical black and yellow stripes. Camels, too, but only sometimes, if it's not raining and is a little late.

Another peculiarity of our walk through the gallery: on all the walks of my life, I've felt with white clarity that I'm the one moving forward and that the thing over which I'm moving is motionless. This time — in addition to my constant forward motion — I felt that the gallery was moving on its own as well, and in the opposite direction. This facilitated our walk, though it didn't speed it up, not for a moment. This feeling, moreover, made me recall those cinematographic film strips that are shot, for instance, from the front of a train: the tracks rushing past with the landscape above them, while one stays still in one's seat, still as the Earth, or rather as the Sun — because it's the Earth that's moving. And I didn't mention this last bit to anyone, not to my wife or the bellhop or any being who may have crossed our path. It was a secret. A secret that swung softly within me, in the opposite direction from my own pendular swinging, so that it hit me regularly in the chest, then in the back — always on the inside, understand. Against my chest, it made the sound of darts snapping; against my back, of fleshy, damp lips stuck together with saliva and blood.

We reached the concierge's desk. Here, the gallery widened along that side, that is, to our right, forming an alcove that was large enough to fit twenty or maybe thirty concierges. But there was only one. Below his ashen mustache, his livery was the color of coagulated bull's blood, shot through with threads of liquid gold that had movable antennae. The concierge paid no attention to them. No surprise there, since — I forgot to mention — they were extremely fine antennae, and no longer than those of a *calluctido-num stridensis*, especially when, under garlands of watchful quails, they sleep with their crystal wings spread wide. This crystal is opaque, with a color somewhere between semen and nearly cooled lava. The same shade appeared in the alcove's windows — because there were stained glass windows all along the back of the alcove. These took the place of what, in the gallery, had been wall panels between semiembedded columns. They shone onto the concierge's entire back half. As such, what I've said about his livery is valid only for his front, which was, moreover, the half we saw. But even though we didn't stop, I could tell — perhaps it is wiser to say I could guess — what color was back there. As we passed, the concierge bowed his head so that the top of his cap, which had been absorbing light from the windows for a long time, came to rest in our visual field. For a second, it retained the color so long received. It was the color of webs woven by viscous, purple-bellied spiders. Then, as if a hand were pulling it upward by a thread, this color slid away and vanished. And the cap became the same color as the livery: coagulated bull's blood.

We passed, all of us. The concierge passed, sucked completely into the light green of his alcove. The stained glass windows darkened. Then the single emerald green wall hanging was reflected in each of the empty panes of glass.

Our pendular swinging increased in amplitude and softness.

There appeared — always to our right — a door pierced by a metal arrow. Obeying its instructions, we left the gallery, following the bellhop and suitcases. And we entered a vast rubber plaza. Some half-dead trees darkened its enormous, hollow silence. Before going on I will say: the inherent color of the trees was olive; in that place, however, it was streaked with glints of bitter ebony.

More or less at the center of the plaza, we stopped. The bell-hop set our suitcases on the ground, where they formed a sort of monolith as tall as my wife. Leather made from the hides of camels, deer and reindeer, cobras, lizards, Indian toads, leopards and lynxes, all curled up in a ball and waited for my wife and me as the bellhop disappeared. Then I looked at the facade of the building we had just left, the great Hotel Mac Quice.

Its walls were the color of dirty clouds. Where the clouds were watery and foretold rain, the walls were a reddish color, a mossy copper. I have seen pavlona flowers in weak sunlight against a blue sky. You have to look at them for a long time and then get bored, without smoking. That was the color of the Hotel Mac Quice's walls.

The surface of the street was like a felled jacaranda trunk, but flat, not round. Footsteps resounded on it like my cough when, in the dark of night, I muffle it with my big strawberry-colored silk handkerchief with steel-gray edging and a yellow diamond in the middle, which I use to stifle my cough so my wife doesn't wake up. For I always watch out for my wife's sleep, and I always have. Otherwise, my wife would never have had a single night of perfect peace, for as long as I can remember, I never gone without a cough pulling me, suddenly, from my dreams, not for a single night. Because I dream. Every night I ravel out the same dream: a gazelle, always the same one, comes to me, comes and goes and bleats at my sex, and the gazelle is an unknown woman. Another second longer and I will recognize her, and I start to hope again that in the future, I will be able to direct my daytime steps in a different way. But the woman screams, a fit of coughing seizes my throat, and I wake up. Then my strawberry, gray, and yellow handkerchief deepens, hollows out the echo of my cough, which resounds in the bedroom like the soft, muffled echo of footsteps on a street made of jacaranda trunks. And my wife can go on sleeping.

That's what the street and the whole plaza where we now stood were like. And there in front of us, the mass of the walls with their

146

thousand windows. Atop a row of them, in worn green letters, the words Hotel Mac Quice.

A feeling of unease started to come over me. Then, slowly, this feeling began to turn into a thought that overtook me entirely: I started to think — with difficulty, it's true — that surely, on leaving our room, something, at least one thing, had been forgotten there. Something, no doubt about it. Needless to say, there was no going on without first checking for and retrieving it.

"One moment," I said.

I crossed the jacaranda trunks and entered the hotel through a side door that left me almost in front of our room, saving me the whole long walk through the plush gallery.

I opened the door, went in, looked around. In effect, we had forgotten: my tortoiseshell toothbrush the shade of artificial orange juice, or more like jelly that was three-fourths orange extract and one-fourth persimmon, the kind my mother used to make twenty years ago to celebrate any family success. On the toothbrush handle it says Garantie. Always, before using it, I would hold this handle up to my left eye and peer through it. All of life, toward the past as well as the future, consisted of jelly that had a tendency to melt, and my mouth tasted, as a result, a whisper of acrid oranges. Every morning I told myself — promised myself — that in the afternoon I would buy a toothbrush with a green tortoiseshell handle so that life would have the flavor of crunching apples. Well, that's not the point. The point is that we had forgotten my toothbrush. We had also forgotten a pair of white suede shoes that my wife wore every other morning; our Voigtlander six-by-nine camera; my straw hat; the bath soap; three of my wife's bras, two pink, the other duck-egg. This last one had a hole at the right nipple. That was no reason to forget it. We had also forgotten her robe, black silk on the outside, milky-white flannel on the inside, with two little ink stains near the collar and another, very dubious stain — so dubious that it had several times occasioned heated arguments, this stain that was almost perfectly round and brownish-gray and located, when the robe was tightly tied and my wife stood motionless in the middle of the room, her eyes gazing at me — oh, what a woman! — located, as I was saying, just two centimeters above the scar from her appendicitis. We had forgotten all of my ties, without exception (except, understand, the one I was wearing and that — as I neglected to say when describing my attire — was the color of parchment that had been partly cleaned, thus harmonizing admirably with my suit and even more so with my hat). But all the rest of them, forgotten! And there were three and a half dozen of them. We had forgotten my wristwatch, a Longines; a tube of aspirin; my tuxedo of English cloth, by Simos, $1,750; a little American oak box with a Chinese lacquer lid containing four unused condoms, Safety Brothers Ltd. brand, made of pigeon eardrums and ranging, the full dozen, from the finest cerulean to the coarsest Prussian blue. Also, our portable Decca phonograph, with two cante jondo records, one by Angelillo and the other by La Niña de los Peines; three Italian operas: *Rigoletto*, *Mephistopheles*, and *Pagliacci*; and one record with "Carmagnole" on one side and "L'internationale" on the other. Also an ashtray advertising Cordon Vert-Champagne Demi-Sec Reims. A tie pin that we had bought the day before as a gift for my uncle Diego, which was a petrified cherry mounted in a platinum claw. We had forgotten a package of food that my wife had carefully prepared. It contained eight sandwiches that we were to have eaten simultaneously, she and I, in four stages: The first two were wild goat cheese, meant to be swallowed while, like pendulums, we advanced through the ochre gallery over the carpeted silence. The next two were to be eaten in the square, one hour later, in front of the hotel; they were smoked shark. The next two an hour later, when we would be in the flat golden countryside; they were wolf-lip sandwiches. Finally, the last two, nightingale-feet sandwiches, were to be consumed as we crossed the threshold of the room that awaited us to shelter our next lovemaking, our mutual sleep, my unidentified gazelle, my jacaranda cough and her pious slumber.

We'd forgotten that package, too. In addition, we'd forgotten our ten-month-old kitten, Katinka. As soon as she saw me enter and gaze in astonishment at all we had forgotten, she came purring over to rub against my pant legs. And we had also forgotten my walking stick made of *latrodectus formidabilis* wood; the paper knife; six packets of Cuban tobacco; a bouquet of azaleas given to us by the hotel owner; my wife's douche; the notes for my next novel; an invitation to a wine exposition; and my tarantula-skin evening slippers with little oil paintings depicting various scenes from the passion and death of Our Lord Jesus Christ. And we had forgotten my sister María, who was still in her silky paper pajamas, softly sleeping under lightweight sheets as if nothing had happened. María slept with infinite innocence, and was surely traversing beautiful dreams, because beside her, surrounding the whole bed, hung a vague perfume of reheated agate. The corners of her mouth trembled.

We had forgotten all of that.

I didn't feel strong enough to gather up so many things, mostly because I was assaulted by the idea that as I was gathering them up, my eyes would fall upon even more forgotten things. And it could very well be an endless affair. So I summarily waved a hand, thought, "Forget all that!" and through the same side door, went back out to the plaza.

My wife had gone.

My wife had taken off with all the suitcases. She hadn't left a single one, not one, to mark the place where just a second before we had been together, united and silent.

She was gone.

I sat on a bench of soft wood, facing the hotel walls. The color of the bench's planks was somewhere between avocado pit and baked clay. As I stared at the hotel's letters, their color was streaked, for brief moments, with skull blue.

There was no one in the plaza or in any of the streets that led to it.

I waited for half an hour. No one. I waited an hour. No one. At one hour and seventeen minutes of bench sitting, a man went by. He was dressed in black, his hands in his overcoat pockets, his hat low on his head. His neck was wrapped in a scarf that was also black, but had some threads of silver-gray. He walked quickly past, taking little steps. This man, no doubt about it, knew where he was going. He epitomized, with his overcoat, his pulled-down hat, his scarf and hurried walk, all the hope that I could hold. So I followed him. There was a stretch of some five or six meters between us. No more.

He turned into one alley, then another and another, always quickly.

The streets here were not like those of our normal cities, where, to turn from one into another you must rotate ninety degrees or else risk continuing indefinitely along the same street. Here, the streets and alleys were tortuous and tangled, so that although the man in question was constantly turning from the one to rush down the other, he always maintained a single direction — always that way, to the east. I don't think he ever deviated more than fifteen or twenty degrees from his target. Of course, he would then use the city's topography to correct for those fifteen or twenty degrees, and if he again deviated a little in the opposite direction, he would find a way to point his face back toward his goal in the east.

These streets and alleys had no color, because I was looking only at my man ahead of me. Clearly, if some vibrant color had suddenly appeared in them — an emerald green, for example, like the hanging in the gallery, or scarlet, or orange, etc. — my eyes would have registered it, and, on registering it, would have focused on it, and, thus focused, would have noticed that streets and alleys, like everything else, had color. But there was nothing vibrant. So the only concession I can make is that it was all grayish or ashen. That's all.

We walked like that for a long time. Finally, a lightening in the near distance let me know we were approaching a clearing that was more open than this maze of jumbled houses. In effect, with a few more steps, we entered a plaza with some nearly dead trees. The man sat down on a bench. I sat next to him, but not right next to him. Since the bench was quite long, I left a few meters between us. In front of us was a big building with a thousand windows. There, in large, faded, gold and green letters, it said Hotel Mac Quice. Naturally, when I read these letters, I judged it necessary to put a little order into my ideas and above all into my actions, for this lay completely beyond anything I was accustomed to.

I lurched between various murky assumptions, until a light — somewhat doubtful, a bit opaque — shone in my mind: the man, exploiting the city's circuitousness, had not walked always toward the east, but — without my realizing — had made a big circle and returned to the plaza by way of the street opposite the one he had taken to leave it.

After a short rest, the man stood up and resumed his walk. He started down the same street as the previous time. I took my place six meters behind him, and off we went!

To keep the thing from happening again, I immediately took certain precautions. Just above our walk, a faded star was twinkling. I looked at it carefully. There was no way to get confused. Two other stars paled below it, forming a triangle; above, somewhat to the right, was a fourth one, vaguely reddish. What's more, those four stars were the only ones shining, at least in that sector of the sky. What could I confuse them with? As further precaution, I consulted my pocket compass: good! North to my left, south toward the hotel, west piercing my belly, east behind the man under the four stars. And so, off we went!

We walked, walked, walked. My eyes went from the man to the stars, from the stars to the compass, from the compass to the man. The alleyways twisted a little from time to time. If the man curved to the right, the stars, to compensate, heeled like a ship's mast to the same degree toward the left. And, so that everything obeyed will of the Supreme Maker or his cardinals, my needle, in its circle, brushed the nipple on the side of my heart.

Then the man corrected his trajectory. The stars hung above us and the needle moved away from me, now perpendicular to my left side. And when the man swerved the other way, the same thing repeated on the right side, rhythmically, the four tiny lights winking up there against the sky.

We walked without changing our direction. We walked eastward. Until, after a long walk, we reached the clearing of a large plaza. Half-alive trees, long benches, jacaranda. In front of us, thick letters: Hotel Mac Quice.

The order I'd given to my ideas the last time was now crumbling. To think that the stars themselves would shift according to our direction would have been absurd. Same for the compass. Another explanation was needed. Any other, so long as it was different.

I could find only one. It is this: a new concept of urban aesthetics.

Why not? I, for my part, had always dreamed of arranging large buildings and city centers differently, and, as such, the arteries that joined them. My dream cities were rounded; their maps would be great round filigrees. Well, it could be that a different sort of plan had been realized here, at least based on what I had seen so far. A long plan, with the city's large hotels placed over its length at regular intervals. For greater harmony, all these hotels would look the same, and so would the plazas in front of them. For the utmost expression of this harmony, they would all have the same name: Mac Quice. Why not? No other explanation came to me. And the man started walking again.

Colorless alleys, stars, compass. The man entered a square, stopped, and sat down. I entered behind him, and, like him, I stopped and sat down. In front of us I read: Hotel Mac Quice.

My concept of a new urban aesthetic wavered.

The man went on. Another square. Hotel Mac Quice.

My concept of a new urban aesthetic wavered.

Hotel Mac Quice.

It wavered; my concept wavered.

Hotel Mac Quice.

Hotel Mac Quice.

Such a concept of urban aesthetics was impossible.

A thing repeated three times over would be magnificent — at least to my taste — but when repeated ten, fifteen, and twenty times, it was an unbearable absurdity.

Fine. That's why men don't repeat, don't extend things, at least not beyond certain very restricted limits. The most solid thing they have, when extended, becomes absurd. They don't do it, no. Thus they don't do it here, either, they couldn't have done it here.

I needed to find another explanation. It was this:

The solution was that, between plaza and plaza, hotel and hotel, we went all the way around the world, no more and no less.

There is on this Earth no more than one single plaza with dying trees and jacaranda echoes. There is on this Earth only one Hotel Mac Quice.

That's the solution.

The man has taken a seat for the fifty-fifth time. Fifty-fifth ... It is time (long past time!) to definitively find out what's going on. For there could be still another solution. It remains within the realm of possibility. It is time — instead of continuing this guesswork — to cut straight to that solution, if it exists. That is, it's time to ask the man.

Two meters between us. I gently slide toward him. Between us, no more than half a meter. We must start a conversation.

I thought first of all about the color it would have. I gathered in my brain all the information at hand: place, time, circumstances, etc. Our conversation would be the color of pure water in a bluish crystal glass, with a final ray of orange sunlight falling nearby, surrounded by air trapped in stone.

Whatever the color, though, I could not break the silence by saying to my friend, "Sir, let us talk, and if we talk, all that we say ..." and the rest I've already mentioned.

Better to leave aside everything related to color and go straight to the matter under discussion.

But here my choices seemed to bristle with problems. The topic had to be something not very far removed in time; to this man, no doubt, events became shrouded in indifference as they withdrew into history. Something of pulsing actuality, then ... but pulsating actuality always has a doubtful, suspicious side; it can be used to trip one up, to saddle one with a commitment. And then ...

The man got up and walked off down the same alley. We walked. We reached a rubber square; our footsteps echoed like jacaranda trunks; on walls of dirty clouds and pavlona flowers were the words: Hotel Mac Quice.

I sit.

Something about my private life, then, my struggles and woes: my wife's disappearance or the thousand things forgotten in the hotel room. Start there? Surely. Because there is only one Hotel Mac Quice on the entire planet Earth. But the fact is that a man who starts in on his private life from out of nowhere only flaunts his mediocrity, his shameful weakness. And it goes without saying that such a man cannot be given information, cannot be granted knowledge about a matter as complex and above all as deep as the one that occupied and tormented me.

There is the weather to be talked about, the muffled colors that lay over plazas, hotels, whole cities. But the man would think: "This character has followed me for over fifty-six plazas only to talk to me, in the end, of things like this ... A fool, no doubt about it!"

Fifty-seven!

And to talk, just talk, about *whatever*? *Whatever*, when it is spoken of, is not located in history — it is permanent. *Whatever* is unrelated to private life, it floats above men without penetrating to their marrow. Oh! But now I think that anything can be *whatever*, depending on the face of the speaker and that of the listener. And I cannot be sure of anything about my face once something is uttered, once the utterance moves away from my lips, and, especially, if it is the color of pure water, bluish crystal glass, orangish sun, stony air. How to know whether I can respond to another's face when I'm on the receiving end of such things!

Fifty-eight!

But what is always talked about, what everyone talks about, spontaneously. When one speaks, one speaks of, one speaks of …

Fifty-nine!

I cough, search my brain, listen to the entire country's speech and get tangled up in the cogs of its language. Come on! Hurry!

Sixty!

Speak, speak, speak …! Come on!

"Sir …" I began. Cough. My large handkerchief of strawberry, steel, and gold flashed before my eyes. The gazelle. Its dream.

"Sir …" The world was now chaos to me.

"Sir, what do you think of Marcel Proust?"

Upon hearing my question, his tie went pale.

Now he leaves, going down the same alleyway. I grab hold of the bench of silvered bone and baked clay, and cling to it. Sink my nails into it. As my friend walks away, I feel like my chest is being sucked out through my clothes.

He is gone. My chest returns.

Now, what if I just went in a different direction?

With slow steps, turning my back to the hotel's walls, I walked away. I passed beneath the half-dead trees. From below, their streaks of bitter ebony were Sienese browns streaked in turn with chalk-gray.

I went on. The alleyways down which I walked had much of this chalk. Once, hanging from a balcony, there was a peach-colored oriental cloth. Another time, from another balcony, an orchid fell.

Suddenly, between three or four houses, a small plaza opened up. At its center, a fountain whispered. At the back, a small hotel. Its milky-white walls oozed a puma-skin sheen. Old lead letters read Hotel O'Connor.

Its windows were of an extremely bright Veronese green. One of them opened wide, revealing a hole the purple shade of a barrel's depths. Over this shade and edged by the bright green, my wife appeared enframed. When she saw me, she waved a handkerchief of cold violets. I waved back with my old scroll hand.

I went up. One after another, I visited the hotel's fourteen rooms. I cracked open each door, craned my neck and poked my head inside, then withdrew my head without having perceived a soul. Just the rooms. And the rooms — which from outside took on a purple barrel-bottom shade — were thick ink inside. Across from each window was a rectangle, lemon cadmium in its upper three quarters. The lower quarter, reflecting the roofs of the neighboring buildings, was, atop that cadmium, fresh lilac.

No one. Except in one room, an old man wrapped in an earthy robe. When he saw me, he spat at me.

No one else. No sign of my wife.

I went down. Framed in her window, she waved her cold violets.

I went up. No one.

I went down. Always, her cold violets.

I set off in search of the man. I am in search of him. I go on, I'm still searching. At regular intervals I pass the hulk of the Hotel Mac Quice. Minutes later, the small Hotel O'Connor goes by, and my wife, from her window, waves at me.

There is no sign of the man. Just now a question has come to me, a supposition: perhaps I can't see him because he is behind me.

A matter of turning my head?

Surely. But what would I gain with the knowledge that he is or is not behind me?

Hotel Mac Quice.

Hotel O'Connor.

Hotel O'Connor.

Hotel Mac Quice.

The Cantera Estate

FOR INFORMATION ABOUT THE CANTERA ESTATE, please consult agent E. Buin. Office: tenth floor of the Pacific Bank, any working day, during working hours. Very unusual not to find him there. He only takes fifteen days off, in the middle of summer.

But all this belongs to another book — *Miltín 34*, if I remember correctly.

I, for my part, cannot provide any greater detail. And yet:

The property measures 849 square blocks, of which 208 are richly fertile and naturally irrigated, 33 are artificially irrigated, 191 are gentle slopes suitable for livestock, and 417 are hills that can be used for seasonal farming. Spacious living quarters, administration buildings, storehouses, two silos, nine tenant properties of galvanized iron and sixteen made of black iron, a large dairy barn, a vegetable garden, fruit orchards, poplar and eucalyptus plantations. Mortgage debt: $350,000.

The Cantera Estate has all this, as well as cattle, horses, sheep, hogs, and domestic fowl. For further details, consult E. Buin.

It has all that.

When I arrived at the aforementioned estate (April 1, 1935; 6:20 p.m.), I noticed that it had something else: a marked discontent.

Discontent drifted down through the leaves of the trees and dominated all the inhabitants of the houses and the fields.

I felt an immediate need to remedy this evil, which came from an incipient putrefaction of the soul. The best remedy was a process of repeating the most orderly foundations upon which our life as men rests.

There were three of us as the sun began to set: Desiderius Longotoma (a prudent and wise man), Julián Ocoa (a distinguished violinist), and me.

All three of us were wearing black frock coats buttoned to the neck with top hats and black gloves. We stood side by side, our elbows touching.

And we started forward resolutely, but gradually separated at an angle of thirty degrees.

In front of each of us — at a distance of 125 meters — there was something:

In front of Longotoma, a pile of bricks;

in front of Ocoa, a folding ladder;

in front of me, a pear tree.

We advanced in a military march. Until we arrived: Longotoma at the pile, Ocoa at the ladder, me at the pear tree.

Halt! A single minute. And then we climbed at the same time.

At the top, we watched the sun disappear. When it was gone, Longotoma doffed his hat, and, raising it up, exclaimed, "1, 2, 3, 4, 5, 6, 7 — 7, 6, 5, 4, 3, 2, 1."

And he donned his top hat again and was silent.

Then Ocoa made the same gesture and said, "Do, re, mi, fa, sol, la, ti, do — ti, la, sol, fa, mi, re, do."

And he donned his hat and was silent.

Then, imitating them, I pronounced, "A, B, C, D, E, F, G — G, F, E, D, C, B, A."

And I donned my hat and was silent.

We came down simultaneously, and again, 125 meters in the opposite direction, approaching at a thirty-degree angle until we were elbow to elbow, our backs to the place where the sun had hidden.

It grew dark. But a little sun dust remained: greens on the leaves, ochres on the ground, reds on the flowers. An old, hunched man with a broom and dustpan gathered it all up. He tossed it onto his cart, and off he went with the sun's remains. When he turned behind some storehouses, night fell.

Night fell, and it was a metal night.

Each of our minds burned with faith in the return of basic order, and, as a result, the departure of all discontent.

II

METAL NIGHT.

Past the houses there is a vineyard, bordered in the daytime by an adobe wall.

I'm now wearing white pants, a dark blue jacket, and no hat.

I stop in the middle of the vineyard, certain that in front of me, no more than twenty steps away, *he* is there.

I turn around and go back. He, then, turns around and walks away.

I stop. He stops.

I turn, he turns. I walk forward, he walks forward. We get closer. Until there are twenty steps between us. I stop, he stops.

Desiderius Longotoma has gone to his room and is reading: Plutarch — *Parallel Lives.*

Julián Ocoa, under an oak tree, has picked up his violin and is playing: Debussy — *Petite Suite.*

I look into the night and have the following feeling: the vertigo of peril.

Violin notes reach me. Longotoma's voice purrs: "The family of Cato derived its first luster from his great-grandfather Cato . . ."

Peril, because I know that if we close by even a centimeter the distance that now keeps the two of us in two separate worlds, our atmospheres will mix into one and we will be bound by it, I know.

Ocoa trills.

Longotoma: "... He afterward followed Brutus, to whom he was very faithful and very serviceable, and died in the field of Philippi."

Then, as I turn, *he* will not turn in turn, since he will follow me. And if I run, he will chase me.

I will tire first, and he will catch up to me from behind.

I turn around and go back.

He turns around and leaves.

Metal night. It grows darker, slowly, old copper.

III

I ALWAYS HAVE IN MIND THE TIME SHOWN ON MY watch at that moment: ten o'clock sharp.

Never in all my life has the knowledge so acquired done me any good, and at that precise moment, the only thing that occurred to me when I saw the watch's hands, was that all throughout my country the clocks were showing ten, but in the neighboring country they were already pointing at eleven. On the other hand, nine was shown nowhere, since it fell in the middle of deserted waters, unless just then an errant little boat was passing through.

Not very likely.

IV

A MOMENT LATER, ALL THE ANTHILLS IN THE REGION exploded. And their galleries, which for centuries had imprisoned the ants, flew through the air with a sound like glass birds.

When that happened, I was overcome by a fear that those explosions would bring about a new and formidable disorder that would cause the whole Cantera Estate to collapse.

I ran.

There was no danger at all, because there were Desiderius Longotoma and that cynic Valdepinos.

Julián Ocoa had perished.

There were many friars carrying his body. On his chest, the violin; on his legs, the bow.

The cortege advanced slowly. In front, a cross swayed like the mast of an errant little ship in the middle of deserted waters at nine o'clock at night.

Parallel to and in the opposite direction of the cortege ran all the rats of Cantera and all the ants that had lost their anthills.

There was no danger at all.

V

DESIDERIUS LONGOTOMA AND THAT CYNIC VALDEPI-nos were there.

Julián Ocoa had perished.

RIP

The two men were in a vast warehouse. All the light was umber, the color of sawdust in a circus ring. The ebony center table, the white chairs, the round blue marble, the two men, all umber, the faded umber of a kerosene lamp. And so, when I took a strawberry from my pocket, a beautiful harmony of colors formed between the strawberry and everything else.

Desiderius Longotoma, aside from being prudent and wise, is short, fat, and moustachioed. The cynic Valdepinos, aside from being cynical, is tall, thin, and clean-shaven.

They were sitting together at the table, one across from the other. The two of them swayed alternately in rhythm: when one leaned forward until his forehead touched the table, the other straightened up until his eyes fixed upon the ceiling. And this, with an absolute, fixed rhythm. Thus, all that they and the place emitted was pure harmony, harmony capable of defying all the explosions in the world.

And rhythm and harmony will only grow once you add the following: in each movement, Valdepinos said, "*Tinguiririca*"; and Longotoma said, "Melan*cho*lic as a *hur*ricane *lamp*."

Bum, bum,

      bum, bum ...

Absolute rhythm. Pure harmony.

"*Tin*guiri*ri*ca."

"Melan*cho*lic as a *hur*ricane *lamp*."

So much harmony and rhythm set my nerves on edge. And as they were set on edge, the round blue marble began to move.

It started to roll around on the floor, and, occasionally, to bump into my feet.

And so, very quietly, I left.

It was fortifying to know — in spite of my nerves — that those two men were there, in the umber light, giving order to everything that could fall into disarray.

VI

AS I CROSSED THE THRESHOLD:

"The widow!" I cried out, and rightly so, since the damned pointy old woman was coming at me like a missile.

"Oh, my dear!" she said, "I was such great friends with your parents ..."

And she made me rewind seven years of my life.

"I bet you don't even remember when we were all living on calle Chuquisaca..."

And she pushed me thirty years back.

"Oh, my dear," she repeated, hanging from my lapel now, "you used to call me Aunty Chacha..."

Lord Almighty! I was clinging to this world by a mere two years.

"And if you only knew how I always remember that day, the year when..."

The old witch! Now she's stuck me back in my mother's womb!

"I'll tell you, dear, that when I was a little girl just like your niece and I played with your mother, who was also a child..."

Sinister old woman, born of Hell! Look at you, happy here in the world of nonbeing, huddled like a sinister squawking al-wakedeka!

"I remember it all, ma'am, all of it, Aunty Chacha ... Here, take five pesos."

VII

I WENT ON THROUGH THE NIGHT AMID BRAMBLES AND weeds, leaving widow and warehouse behind. Until I found myself in front of two veterans who were talking and leaning against the last apple tree.

Since the war of '79, they always talk there.

Now they were discussing an approaching war against some neighboring country, and how they believed in us and our ability to achieve another victory like their own. I listened to them from behind a cherry tree.

Then they spoke of future wars and conquests, when I — according to my calculations — would in turn be a veteran propped against an apple tree at night. And, fired up by bugles, one of them pointed a valiant finger at a boy going past, and, with a martial look, said to the other, "You can be sure, comrade, that when the grandchildren of that lad there ..."

When the lad's grandchildren ...

But, what about me, then, what about me? Just because I'm behind a cherry tree, does my existence flash by like a bolt of lightning?

VIII

I WENT ON LEAPING OVER BRAMBLES AND WEEDS.

When I stumbled against a rock I felt blood flowing from my skin. I was, as such, at the mercy of any evil intention running loose through the fields. And even worse than exposing one's nerves or brain or heart to the power of such intentions, is exposing one's blood to whatever might be roaming on a night given over to all those intentions.

Danger the first.

The second:

With my blood like that, I could also fall prey to any living being, harmless as it may be. For a touch would be enough to make my blood gush through my skin, in thin downward-flowing sheets.

Nothing happened to me, except for the passing of a silent airplane, which, rather than happening to me, happened to all the crickets in the area.

I arrived at the main patio naked; naked not just to the eye, but to all creation.

Not a shred of metal night remained. Now, the night was coal.

In the middle of it, rising from the patio, grew a tube. Its walls were made of air. These walls held the coal-colored night outside of them.

Inside, then, a leaden light dripped down to fill the tube.

Thanks to which I could see that everyone was there, chatting in small groups.

My blood was still exposed.

We chatted without danger.

Until I looked toward one end of the patio:

There, two pretty ladies with wide crinolines inflating the silk of their pink skirts, two pretty ladies, silent and smiling, were looking at me. And the two pretty ladies had faces of wax.

The three of us looked at one another for a second. And my blood, openly, wet my entire body.

The wax of their pretty little faces smiled. The silk of their skirts swished very sweetly.

Two parasols, held by their gloved little hands, framed their two smiles, as well as the black needles of their eyes turned toward me.

There could be no more than ten meters between us.

Behind me, all the meters of my life gone by.

But in front, I repeat, only ten.

I wasn't about to use them up walking toward those ladies. Any man, when he sees he has no more than ten meters left, stops.

Then a soft wind blew then and the patio's mayten trees flickered. The wind took the stretch I refused to walk and walked it back toward me. The two parasols flickered, too, the waxen faces smiled wider, and the gloved ladies, two wide skirts of pink silk sweetly swaying, began to advance delicately toward me in a hushed minuet.

At their approach, I pleaded with all the Gods to unfurl more leagues of life in other directions, even if they led through the surrounding night. But my plea dwindled away and my body was reduced to external threads of blood, threads that circulated outside my skin, outside my will, open — yes! — to all creation, to the breeze in the maytens, to the ladies' kiss, to the contact of their hard lips on my unraveled veins.

Pretty and rhythmic little ladies! Their four little needle eyes were gazing at my neck beneath my ears, and toward that spot they walked. One to either side, they would sink the wax of their faces into my spilled blood and I would feel, on my neck, at that sharply sensitive point, their black lips, solid and defined, as they'd kiss me, kiss me, and I'd enter into them with my whole being — erased into nothingness, into anguished suffocation — through their lips on my neck, while they, intoxicated, would let their two parasols tilt like two flowers drooping from the weight of blood on their silk petals.

Silence! Stillness! Everyone static! Only the bells of their skirts swayed drowsily. I closed my eyes a moment. When I opened them again, the two faces were there beside, beside, beside me, approaching my blood and staring at me. But they were no longer smiling. Serious, inscrutable, impenetrable, they were two masks of quietude: I no longer saw my conversation partners, I no longer saw the patio or its maytens, I no longer saw the ladies' pink skirts, their parasols or their gloved little hands, and my whole being became nothing more than the sight of their motionless, waxy pallor. And now, touching the skin of my blood, they kept coming closer, ever closer, more and more, until, at an absolute standstill, their faces were likewise erased, and for a moment there existed only my two eyes dilated by terror, and their four black, staring eyes, alone in space, piercing mine.

Pretty ladies! It was my final moment.

Then I made a grotesque grimace and laughed.

My laughter hit their pretty faces. And they — sensitive to my mirth — echoed it by laughing in turn, lazily, it's true, but also lackadaisically tipping their torsos backwards.

Then I saw them again, dear little masks, again I saw the pink silk skirts, their brittle swish, the ever-chatting friends, the patio, the maytens, and there, above the rooftops, the last leaves of an aged avocado tree. And then, too, as I saw everything again, I was able to take the measure of my danger, for while the two ladies went on looking at me like that, one of them, unbeknownst to me, had begun to quietly lower her parasol over me, like a fishbowl that would cover me and isolate me from any possibility of existence, enclosing me alone with my blood and their two hard little mouths fitted there behind my ears.

But they were laughing and leaning back, and as they moved away, opening up like a fan unfolding — the instant of my salvation tolled.

I waved my arms and slipped away.

Pretty little ladies of soft wax and pretty silks!

IX

I SLIPPED AWAY, GATHERING MY BLOOD BACK INSIDE me with both hands, placing the skin between it and the air, until I reached the edge of that night on the Cantera Estate.

Then I peered over.

Below, far below, with the muffled sound of rapids, the nights and days went by, intertwined in their holy succession of infinitude.

There below, they slid — light, dark; gold, red — like streamers of the Sun and the Moon, adhering to their mission, with all men inside them, with all their miseries, their good fortunes and their corpses.

To return! To return! That was my hope.

I leapt into the abyss. Behind me, the damned Cantera Estate, tangled up in that detached night wandering the void!

Behind and goodbye to all that!

Now I was swaying as I fell. I heard the whistle of a night passing below me; then the thunder of a day that followed its destiny; and another night, and another day; the endless ribbon unspooling.

I fell.

X

THE CANTERA ESTATE.

For any and all information, please consult agent E. Buin. Office: tenth floor of the Pacific Bank, any working day, during working hours. Very unusual for him to take vacation.

ONE VICE

The Vice of Alcohol

LAST NIGHT, FROM MY BED, I HEARD THE HOARSE CRY of a woman taking pleasure.

Last night I heard the clock stop two minutes to wait for the Moon, which had likewise stopped in order to watch, in its own shadow on the street, two dogs fighting.

Last night I sang, alone and face up:

I'm heading for my mountains
Going to pray to god
For all these many sorrows
The snow, the wind and sun

I heard my own singing, which is highly absurd.

I also considered it highly absurd how matters of sex are organized on this Earth. Because all beautiful girls should be naked, face up, bound with strong chains, their thighs open, wide open. Then they could be ravaged mercilessly.

But there is no organization at all. At least not as long as the stars don't explain their distances by shrinking them to fit in two hands, and as long as bishops don't wear the mossy green of tranquil swamps.

None of the foregoing is arbitrary. Between these three elements — bound girls, stars, and hypothetical green-garbed bishops — I have always seen an absolute kinship. Which is proven by the fact that I have not written down other elements here, but only those. Now then, if, today and for the past forty-two years, I have not been able to dismantle and explain that kinship with well-organized clarity of mind, that's no proof at all that it doesn't exist. Keep in mind that I cannot illuminate each of the elements that form this kinship, yet no one doubts their reality. I defy anyone to dismantle and explain a girl, even if he has tied her up himself. I defy anyone to give a convincing explanation of the stars, even if one has all the telescopes in the world at his disposal, for the telescopes themselves will need an explanation, since they only exist because of the abstract explanation that the brain manufactured beforehand. I defy any human to take a bishop, remove his usual raiment, and replace it with one the exact shade of moss in a tranquil swamp. Then, sit face-to-face with the bishop — he can smoke or not smoke, take snuff or not, I don't care — and, in a clear voice, explain to me what has really just happened. I defy you! And, on the other hand, let he who doubts the existence of girls, stars, and bishops come forward. For my part, I hope someday to be able to explain all of this properly. Let us continue, then, with questions of sex.

They could have a faster solution, if only we could find pleasure in making love to long strips of velvet. This is not arbitrary, either. Here, I could rehash an argument like the one above. But that would take a lot of time, and it is necessary, even urgent, that soon, before the cry of that woman taking pleasure comes to an end, yes, it is indispensable that all well-bred men, all who are moved by the call of Nation and Virtue, yes, it's imperative that we fight tenaciously against the vice of alcohol.

But for that we need a slender boy with dark skin and light eyes, whom we would dress in a very tight bathing costume the color of almond bark and top off with a large hat, a hat that would be planetary, in and of itself and in its grandeur as a whole. Oh, what a magnificent, superb thing a hat is!

Here at home, I have seventeen of them. I solemnly swear that for the past nine years I have never gone to bed without urinating several drops on each of them. Then I pick up a small parlor pistol and fire on the seventeen of them, one after another. Let's get back to the boy.

Unimaginable hat!

The boy will have to wait a few minutes.

I have taken a paraffin box made of unfinished wood. It has five sides. That is, it has one empty side that I cover with a pane of glass so that you cannot touch what's inside, but you can see it. OK.

On one side there are five bottles that increase in size as they get further away from the glass. On the other side are another five just like them. They meet at the back. Like so:

On the first two is written *Beer*; on the second two, *Wine*; on the third pair, *Pisco*; on the fourth, *Whiskey*; on the fifth, *Grain alcohol*.

Symbolic meaning:

The bottles grow in size: the alcoholic needs more and more alcohol.

As the bottles grow, so too does the percentage of alcohol in their contents.

Symbolic meaning:

The alcoholic not only needs a greater quantity, but also increased potency, moving from beer to grain alcohol.

In the foreground, in the center, stands an artificial rose. Like so:

Symbolic meaning:

Under the influence of alcoholic vapors, we see everything as rose-colored, like a rose. Hence the rose.

But the rose is artificial.

Symbolic meaning:

None of what we see as rose-colored is, really, that color. Life goes on. Life is black.

From above, over the rose, hanging from its thread, a hairy tarantula. Like so:

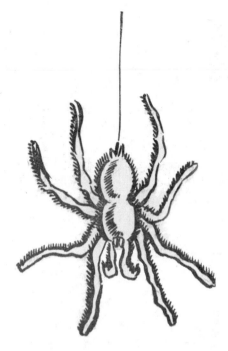

Symbolic meaning:

Tarantulas, especially hairy ones, are repugnant, disgusting, infernal. That is what the vice of alcohol does: it turns you into a repugnant, disgusting, and infernal being.

Do not forget that the tarantula is above the rose.

Symbolic meaning:

The truth is above the lie.

Anyone can make this symbolic construction in their own home. But, if you want it to reach the masses, something else is needed:

The boy!

And the hat.

The boy with his hat must stand behind the box and the box must be placed in the center of a public square. The boy must shout, "Come one! Come all!"

Then, indeed, the crowds will come, and when they see all that, they will forever flee the vice of alcohol.

If men did not drink, perhaps it would be possible to tie up a few girls and savage them. Then the stars could follow their path, the bishops could keep their standard cassocks, and velvet strips could have no fear of being raped.

But the hat is needed. I will accept all models that are sent to me.

Last night I heard the hoarse cry of a woman taking pleasure.

Then the wind blew. It carried away everything. It blew away a bishop and set him down, after eight centuries of flight, in the middle of the Milky Way.

There, that bishop can be our representative in the tenacious fight against the vice of alcohol. Only ... we'll have to find a way to send him a slender, dark-skinned, light-eyed boy as soon as possible. The bishop will take care of dressing him properly once he's arrived. Perhaps, given the climate, in sand.

In any case, we must fight! In the end — don't forget! — there are the chained-up girls. Don't forget: you'll be able to savage them mercilessly!

Last night I heard the hoarse cry of a woman taking pleasure.

A moment later I drank a glass of grain alcohol. And I cried over the misfortunes that afflict my fellow men.

Then I drank a glass of whisky. I wept over how the birds and animals of our planet suffer at the hands of my fellow men.

Then I drank a glass of pisco. I wept for the reptiles, fish, and insects.

Then, a glass of wine. I wept for flowers, leaves, and fruits, for the roots that are buried underground.

Finally, I drank a glass of beer. And I wept for our brothers, our sweet, tender brothers who neither speak, nor grow, nor fornicate: minerals.

Then I commended myself to the bishop of the Milky Way and implored him to ask the Almighty Creator to drop upon the Earth an abundant rain of water from His Kingdom, or else from the regular clouds if the tedium of that moment overcame him.

It rained.

I reached out my two hands pressed together. I leaned over them. I drank, I drank water, innocent and heavenly water.

Lassette appeared, slow, steady, atop her precipitous red little heels.

Smiling, she let me bind her with strong chains.

Naked, pale, far from any shadow of alcohol. Pale, diaphanous. Her hair of gold, ancient and dark; her sex of quivering gold. Her feet with the two long, bloody drops of her heels. The mute chains.

I savaged her mercilessly.

I savaged her with a whip made of horse leather. A tame, peaceful horse. The one who, when I was a very little boy, carried me at a slow gait over the first hill it saw.

I savaged her again and again.

Then the whole neighborhood, all of Santiago, all of Chile, all the Americas heard, in the middle of the night, the hoarse cry of a woman taking pleasure.

JUAN EMAR (1893–1964) is the pen name of the Chilean writer, painter, and art critic Álvaro Yáñez Bianchi. Born in Chile in 1893, he was a strong advocate of the artistic avant-garde of the 1920s and '30s, and his critical writings helped revolutionize the art scene in his country. Underappreciated in his time, he is now considered to be one of the most important twentieth-century Latin American writers.

MEGAN McDOWELL lives in Santiago, Chile. She has translated many of the most important contemporary Spanish-language authors, including Alejandro Zambra, Samanta Schweblin, Mariana Enríquez, and Lina Meruane. She has been nominated four times for the International Booker Prize, and was the recipient of an Award in Literature from the American Academy of Arts and Letters. She won the National Book Award in translation alongside Samanta Schweblin for *Seven Empty Houses*.

CÉSAR AIRA was born in Coronel Pringles, Argentina in 1949, and has lived in Buenos Aires since 1967. Aira has published more than one hundred books to date. In addition to winning the Formentor Prize, he has received a Guggenheim Fellowship and was shortlisted for the Rómulo Gallegos Prize and the Booker International Prize.